BLACKMAIL

Skye Fargo knew better than to get involved with Julia Driscoll. If the hellfire preacher, Brigham "Brimstone" Blutcher, found out Skye had touched the voluptuous widow, he'd make sure Skye was out of a job, leaving the wagon train headed for sure death.

The trouble was, it was damn hard to think straight when Julia stripped off her dress and came to him naked in the pond.

It got even harder when she kissed him and let her hand caress his body.

"Cut it out," Skye protested huskily. "Everybody must know you've left. They'll worry, come looking. If we got caught by old Brimstone or—"

"Then don't make me raise a loud stink, like I do when I don't get my way," Julia said. "Oh, kiss me, kiss me."

At this point the Trailsman had to admit defeat. Julia had him just where she wanted him—and he had trouble acting like it was a bad place to be. . . .

D1409036

THE TRAILSMAN 66

TREACHERY PASS

by

Jon Sharpe

A SIGNET BOOK

NEW AMERICAN LIBRARY

NAL BOOKS ARE AVAILABLE AT QUANTITY DISCOUNTS
WHEN USED TO PROMOTE PRODUCTS OR SERVICES.
FOR INFORMATION PLEASE WRITE TO PREMIUM MARKETING DIVISION,
NEW AMERICAN LIBRARY, 1633 BROADWAY,
NEW YORK, NEW YORK 10019.

The first chapter of this book previously appeared in *River Kill*, the sixty-fifth book in this series.

SIGNET TRADEMARK REG. U.S. PAT. OFF. AND FOREIGN COUNTRIES
REGISTERED TRADEMARK—MARCA REGISTRADA
HECHO EN CHICAGO, U.S.A.

SIGNET, SIGNET CLASSIC, MENTOR, ONYX, PLUME, MERIDIAN
AND NAL BOOKS are published by NAL PENGUIN INC.,
1633 Broadway, New York, New York 10019

First Printing, June, 1987

1 2 3 4 5 6 7 8 9

PRINTED IN THE UNITED STATES OF AMERICA

The Trailsman

Beginnings ... they bend the tree and they mark the man. Skye Fargo was born when he was eighteen. Terror was his midwife, vengeance his first cry. Killing spawned Skye Fargo, ruthless, cold-blooded murder. Out of the acrid smoke of gunpowder still hanging in the air, he rose, cried out a promise never forgotten.

The Trailsman, they began to call him, all across the West: searcher, scout, hunter, the man who could see where others only looked, his skills for hire but not his soul, the man who lived each day to the fullest, yet trailed each tomorrow. Skye Fargo, the Trailsman, the seeker who could take the wildness of a land and the wanting of a woman and make them his own.

Idaho Territory. Late autumn, 1861—
winter already whispering along the Oregon Trail,
that rutted, bloodstained wilderness route
that killed or cured . . .

1

The two puffs of smoke had quickly turned to pale-blue rings, slowly blowing through the mud-chinked windows in the rear wall of the long room. The shrieks and bellows of half-drunken song, the wailing of fiddles, and the pounding of dancing feet had suddenly stopped. The participants could only stand and gape, amazed at the two fast shots that had so suddenly and unexpectedly turned the gaiety into silence.

However, Fat Dan's Grand Slam Casino was used to such upsets. A large, square building of mud, log, and stone, it perched on the south bank of the Snake River with the dozen or so other structures comprising Glenns Ferry. The settlement was well located to serve as a trading post and a natural stop along the Oregon Trail, which forded the Snake here to continue northwestward. Fat Dan's was among the first, begun in the '40s as an honest tavern, changing owners and names but growing steadily on into those hectic '50s, its notoriety growing with it, until it had become one of the most dangerous dives on the far frontier. But despite all it had seen, this latest shooting had been swift enough to make men's hair stand on end.

Across the table in the left-rear corner, a burly gambler lay sprawled forward, his whiskery face resting in a large pile of gold coins and poker chips. Five rumpled cards were tightly gripped in his left hand, the right hand still a balled fist around the cow-horned butt of a double-barreled German pistol.

Against the wall stood the dead gambler's opponent, smoking Colt revolver in hand, calmly viewing the situation. "Counting the joker, a man might make five, but hell if there's a poker deck that packs six aces." His tone lifted only slightly as he glanced toward the long, hewn-log bar. "Houseman, cash me in. A thousand four hundred dollars, in gold. I'm not fond of picture money."

There was no answer for at least ten seconds. Fat Dan's manager and cashier stood by the bar as if transfixed, a slight, thinly gray-bearded man who knew he was damned if he did and damned if he didn't. Death rarely struck just one blow in the Grand Slam Casino. Gazing at the balcony above the bar, he called with relief, "Well, Mr. Tobin?"

Men from the Missouri to the mouth of the Columbia River had heard of Fat Dan Tobin. Fortyish, he was big of bone and flesh like his name, his jowled face sporting a mustache and goatee of the same graying brown as his greasily plastered hair. On his way downstairs when the gunplay erupted, he'd thrust a pudgy hand inside his broadcloth suit coat as if to draw a shoulder-holstered hideout pistol. Removing his hand, he gave the manager a nod and finished his ponderous descent.

The dead gambler was almost as well-known. Many men had tangled with Slick Dudley, who was sharp and shrewd when it came to cards, dice, or wheel, and rumor was that in the two years he'd run Fat Dan's games, Dudley had killed at least a dozen fools who'd bucked his play.

It was impossible that such an operator should die

so quickly at the hands of this stranger. He was black-haired and bearded, his chiseled features darkened by wind and sun, his eyes a cold lake blue that even in this moment of deadly confrontation held an intent reticence, suggesting that he preferred to stand apart. As it was, he stood tall in workaday garb and a buckskin jacket, lean and hard, latent power evident in the relaxed slope of his shoulders. He looked what he was: a rough-hewn, durable, self-sufficient frontiersman—not a backwoods yokel, but not a professional cardshark or gunslinger, either.

Fat Dan Tobin seemed to be taking the stranger's measure, one hand on the staircase post, the other tugging his goatee. Then, after a quick scan around, he spoke in a lazy drawl, devoid of any excitement, "You're wantin' a lot of money, pal. What seemed to be the hassle between you'n Slick Dudley?"

"Too many aces." The stranger's lips twitched as if about to smile. "I caught him three times in a row. He has cards up either sleeve, and I don't know how many you'll find inside his hat. You can shake him down in your leisure. I've said I'm cashing in."

"And yuh called 'im," Tobin replied, ignoring the last remark, "or did yuh just shoot 'im under the table without callin'?"

"I called him. He saw he was trapped and went for his pistol."

"I still say one thousand and four hundred is a lot of money."

"The chips on the table will bear me out." A low hardening was creeping into the stranger's tone. "The deck, the cards in his hand, in his sleeves, and in his hat will prove the rest of it. When you check our hands you'll find that I held a pair of aces and three queens. Slick still holds the king of spades—and four aces."

"Plum interestin', if true." Tobin licked his lips, and again there was silence, faintly broken here and there by the scrape of a boot as the crowd kept easing back to make room. Many of the women who had been dancing or cadging drinks at the bar had already turned and noiselessly scooted away to safer spots. They knew, as did the men, that gunfire would come again, fast and furious, if Fat Dan gave the signal.

One curvaceous wench, though, abruptly deserted her grizzled customer and hurried toward the stairs, her face pale beneath her makeup. She rushed up to Tobin, throwing herself between him and the stranger as she leaned forward, her words intended for a whisper, but they came out as a sharp hiss that carried around the room. "Go easy, honey. Yakima Flynn just told me that man is—"

"Shuddup, Velvet," Tobin growled, shoving her aside and addressing the stranger with a mocking sneer. "Pal, if you'd let Slick Dudley live, we might've settled this thing with no loss o' time. But hell, I ain't about to pay out my good money just 'cause some hotshot kills a gambler at one o' my tables, then rises to make his demand."

As Tobin spoke, the stranger pivoted and triggered his revolver. Another pistol blazed fire across the room, the twin reports drowning out a howl of pain as the casino bouncer reeled against the bar, pawing at his bloodied hand. The long-barreled Adams .44 he'd stealthily drawn clattered to the floor from nerveless fingers, the web of his thumb and much of his palm skewered by lead.

"You're handy, m' friend," Tobin said thickly, then scowled at the woman he'd called Velvet. "Okay, who is he?"

"Skye Fargo."

"Fargo." Tobin regarded the man, tugging his goatee again. "I heard tell o' you. Scout an' pilot for a bunch o' the wagon trains that rolled the trail, weren't you? Raised hell with the Injuns and hard cases around Fort Hall."

"I was there." Fargo's tone was hardening. "Now I'm here, and I'm waiting for my money."

"Wal, 'course if yuh'd made yourself known, sir, no sech misunderstandin' would've ever happened. Not in any place o' mine." Tobin strode to the poker table, making a good show of it, knowing all eyes were on him. With one swift kick he sent the chair flying from under the dead gambler. Slick Dudley's body pitched backward in a loose flop that sprawled itself flat on the floor, arms thrown out, a flutter of cards flying from the sleeves. He stepped astride the corpse and picked up the fine beaver hat, dug a fist into it, and swore.

"Hell," he roared, spilling card after card from inside the hat and tossing it down. "The damn topper's got a double linin' and was stuffed full. Cash Mist' Fargo in, Proust, and have the boys boothill bury this cheatin' carcass. I run an honest house!" As the manager came hustling, Tobin glared at the crowd as if seeking at least a flicker of confirmation from somebody. "Honest Daniel! That's what they used to call me in Kansas. Belly to the bar, folks, the house is buyin' a round. I'll show yuh how big a sport Honest Dan Tobin can be." With that, he stomped back upstairs to his balcony office.

Fargo was relieved, doubting he could've shot his way clear. He was not surprised, though, figuring Tobin's agreeable mood had nothing to do with being honest or a sport, but with getting even and back in control. Might made right on this wild frontier, and a crafty owner of a dive like Fat Dan's would try to gain a hold over anyone strong and skilled. Tobin had simply made a calculated move to whip Fargo into his hands, aware—as Fargo was aware—that a man who would take money, even with the excuse of having won it gambling, was frequently a man who could be handled, shaped, and forced to fight as he was told.

Nor was Fargo surprised to see Velvet start to sidle across the room. The manager, Proust, was piling gold coins on the next table, interested solely in exact counting. But money and power often held a strange fascination for those who plied avaricious trades, and true to type, Velvet was gazing avidly at the stacks as she eased closer, her hand sliding back and forth over her hip.

He kept an eye on her advance while helping Proust sack the money in a canvas string bag, until a man approached and doffed his hat. "M' name's Wyndam, Otis Wyndam. I'm with the wagon train that pulled in this evening. May I set?"

Fargo shrugged and Wyndam settled in a nearby chair, a solid, stout chap of mid-thirties, with one of those homely, frank faces people instinctively trust. He had thinning hair neatly combed, a persuasively earnest voice, and wore plain denims and a butternut shirt; in fact, the loudest thing about him was his hat: a flat sombrero with a braided rattlesnake band, four silver tinsel stars on the crown and four on the underside of the brim. He promptly began a conversation, to which Fargo at first paid only peripheral attention.

"Did I o'erhear correctly, Mr. Fargo, that you're a scout? Yes? And that you've trekked the trail?"

"A time or two, yeah."

"Beyond it, far as the Willamette Valley?"

"South of Portland?" Fargo nodded. "Rich farmland."

"The finest. Sixty- or a hundred-and-sixty-acre tracts, that's my offer to every pilgrim willing to follow me to Oregon City. Virgin soil, deep and fertile, right on the river for transportation, the perfect place to settle new homes. Uh-huh, and the niggardly sum of a dollar an acre is all I'm asking."

"All paid in advance, too, I reckon."

"Ah, well, in this case seeing is believing—" Wyndam choked, Velvet having suddenly intervened with an undulating thrust of her pelvis. Fargo grinned. In her early twenties, he judged, she was in precious little else. Her red spangled dance-hall costume fit like an hourglass corset. She had doe eyes that said she had never loved anyone passionately in her life, and a bee-stung mouth that made liars out of them, especially when she cozied up and planted a kiss on Fargo.

Velvet flashed a saucy look at the openmouthed spectators. "The custom here's for a man to give the girl who kisses him a present, isn't it?" Returning to Fargo, she said, "I'm ready to claim mine, please."

Without a word Fargo pulled Velvet tightly against him and pressed his lips to hers, warmly, lingeringly.

When he released her, she wobbled back a pace and clapped a hand above her breasts, partly because she was gasping for breath and partly because Fargo had discreetly dropped four gold coins down her cleavage during their embrace. A chorus of hoots and guffaws erupted. An embarrassed flush brightening her rouged cheeks, Velvet burrowed through the hurrawing crowd to make a quick getaway out a side door.

Chuckling, Fargo wedged the cash bag behind his belt and was tucking in his shirt when he saw Wyndam glance obliquely at the front entrance. Following, he glimpsed a large, rawboned man in a long frock coat and black slouch hat of the sort worn by parsons. Shocks of white hair showed under the brim, and a wide mattress of beard spread down his brawny bosom, almost bristling as he glowered with righteous condemnation.

When Wyndam faced Fargo again, he realized Fargo had caught his glance and laughed softly, waving his hand. "That's Brigham Blutcher, a member of our train. He doesn't approve of this, or of you." Wyndam paused, thoughtfully studying Fargo. "You're a fiddle-foot rogue, but there's more to you than that. I don't miss on many folks. It's my guess that once you agree to a job, you'd stick through to finish it come Satan or high water. Am I right?"

"If I can. If the job's as agreed." A faint suspiciousness edged his voice. "You ain't hinting your train needs to hire a pilot, are you?"

"Nope. I can guide okay, and our second section is bossed by an ex-teamster who knows the ropes and follows m' lead well. Tremayne's his name. Give him a howdy for me, will you, if you're here when he pulls in next week."

Fargo scowled. "No train has sections strung a week apart."

"It kinda developed. More folks joined than I bargained for, almost forty wagons. Enough to form two sections, luckily, 'cause feuding grew hot 'tween those not ready to leave and thems unwilling to wait. Leaders we got plenty of," Wyndamn added, a harried sigh. "I thought p'raps we might take you on as a wing scout."

"Forget it. If you're smart, forget going at all. You're too late, the season's gone, and signs point to an early, stormy winter. Don't bet your lives on reaching Oregon City before heavy snows block the Blue Mountains, or ice blizzards trap you along the Columbia Gorge."

"We don't intend to. I've got copies of maps Gen'ral Stevens drew when he explored overland to the Pacific Northwest. Detouring on his route will bypass the Gorge and Deadmans Pass, and cut a hundred miles or more off the regular trail—"

Fargo tensed, mouth clamped, eyes narrowing speculatively.

"Still, time is pressing. But so are we, and barring any major delay, I expect we'll succeed." Wyndam finished confidently, then waved the thought away as if it was unimportant. "But this isn't what I wanted to talk to you about. We've had some trouble and we'll have some more. I need a man who can handle vermin the way you just did. It's worth high dollars to me."

Fargo shook his head. "I'm pulling out in the morning."

"Westbound?"

"Wyoming, the Teton Basin." Fargo turned to go with a parting nod. "I hope your train, both halves, makes it across."

Talk had gradually resumed in the casino, but it died again, as Fargo pushed through the crowd toward the big front door. There on the threshold loomed Brigham Blutcher, who straightened and sniffed audibly.

"I seen you. Boozin', gamblin', lechin', spillin' blood! I seen your bloody hands," Blutcher accused dourly. "Beware! The wages of sin is death."

Fargo smiled. "Sure. But you saw me all wrong. I was just helping a certain tinhorn collect what he'd earned."

Outside, the night was cloudy dark, the only illumination coming from lamplit windows. Fargo headed warily along the street toward the local rooming house, pausing in a black-shrouded alleyway to reload and scan ahead for ambushes. Most likely Fat Dan Tobin had a fast recovery scheme cooked up, and a tavern full of hard-ass jiggers also knew what and how he'd won. Instead of reholstering his revolver, Fargo stuck it in his belt to one side of his money bag, butt forward in a loose, left-handed cross-draw position.

Moving on, he passed a few men, none of them close by and none appearing to be taking any special interest in him. He paused again when he reached the lane that led to the rooming house. Hearing nothing, seeing nothing in the gloom, Fargo began down the fetid, narrow alley with utmost caution. It was flanked by hovels and shacks that were mostly dark and silent, although an occasional glimmering window and muffled hum of voices denoted occupancy. Plenty of nooks and doorways and spaces between the shanties provided a killer a place to hide in wait.

He caught no sound, no flicker of motion. Yet danger was here, deadly, silkily whispered danger. The premonition was strong—and proved to be right.

Fargo was halfway down the lane when a shadowy figure leapt out of an alcove doorway ten yards ahead, aiming a sawed-off rifle and snarling loudly, "Fork it over, asshole, or I'll blow you to smithereens!"

As he halted, Fargo swiftly analyzed his chances and decided they were lousy. He grimaced, and it was then he heard a quick, light step behind him. Whirling, he glimpsed another man looming over him from out a concealed side doorway, his arm raised, gripping a butcher knife. That slashed the odds from lousy to zero, which meant Fargo had nothing to lose.

With a sharp twisting of his body to the left, Fargo threw a right forearm block to deflect the slashing blade, and drew his revolver with his left hand, corkscrewing it up and ramming it into the man's gut. He triggered, the blast muffled by meat and bone.

The man's head flew back, striking the doorway, blood fountaining from bullet punctures front and back. His honed steel blade sliced past the corded muscles of Fargo's midriff, snagging his buckskin jacket slightly, then arching harmlessly to land in the dirt.

Dead on his feet, the man began crumpling. Fargo saw the flare of the sawed-off rifle and heard a terrific roar, a slug chipping the wall behind him, and ducked reflexively as he pivoted back to the first man. Too late. Running bootfalls were retreating down the alley, and he realized that the man must've panicked and started to flee the instant he'd seen his partner had failed.

Fargo stood in angry silence, staring at the darkness into which the man had disappeared. Then, turning, he knelt to examine his attacker, who was slumped as if asleep against the wall. The man had ordinary clothes and a few ordinary effects like tobacco and a pencil stub, not much money and no identification. His looks weren't anything worth remembering, either.

Behind Fargo on the main street, a pistol cracked, and then another, the reports coming faintly from the southeast. Here in the alley it was very quiet, the confrontation having been so swift that apparently it had passed unnoticed. Nobody was shouting alarm, nobody was running to see what was wrong; it was almost as if he'd never been stopped here at all.

Fargo left it that way as he strode on to the rooming house.

A standard, two-story whitewashed farmhouse, it perched high on a great multicolored rock mound overlooking the river. Inside, the front room served as a lobby, with bedrooms upstairs and owner's quarters in the rest of the downstairs. The owner's son slept on the sofa in the lobby, and like an obedient watchdog, arose when Fargo entered. Bleary-eyed, he grabbed a key from the pigeonhole rack and tossed it to Fargo.

Fargo shook his head. "I'm in room four. This key is stamped number twelve."

"Don't matter. Any key fits any lock."

"So that's how the mouse got in. You got a trap?"

Sleepily the son rummaged around and found a common catch-spring mousetrap. He apologized for not having bait, calling as Fargo was going up the stairs, "If you're worried about the key, put a chair against the door."

Room Four had a chair, which Fargo promptly wedged under the knob. It also had a humpbacked bed, a tall wardrobe, and a combination bureau and washstand. On the floor were his saddlebags, on the bureau was a hobnail lamp with a tasseled shade, and on the washstand was a bowl and cracked pitcher.

Fargo lit the lamp, drew the windowshade, took his gun-cleaning kit from his saddlebags, and hauled his Sharps rifle out of the wardrobe. Carefully he cleaned the Sharps and loaded a fresh charge, thinking of Fat Dan as he did so. Crossing Tobin was fairly a cut-and-dried affair, with about as much subtlety as a buffalo's prick.

Otis Wyndam and his train, however, now that was bamboozling. Each section made an average-sized train, big enough to provide reasonable security without being unwieldy. Yet trains can be any size; it shouldn't have mattered to Wyndam if more folks joined than he bargained for, and to travel a week apart, because of petty wrangling showed rotten leadership. Still, they'd probably muddle through if winter held off and they didn't detour according to Wyndam's maps. Oh, General Isaac I. Stevens had trailblazed a government railroad survey, all right. But the path he charted in '53 ran far north from upper Montana to Fort Walla Walla on the Washington side of the Columbia River. Otis Wyndam was either stupid or a liar . . . and the land promoter had not looked stupid.

Propping his Sharps by the bed, Fargo decided on a quick cat bath before retiring. He peeled off his clothes and proceeded to wash away the grime. He was working with the towel when he heard someone stop out in the hall, and knuckles tapped softly on his door.

"Hello? Are you awake?"

He recognized Velvet's voice, her whisper pleasant and innocuous enough. But Fargo had been lured before by sweet-sounding traps, and instinctively he checked that the shade and lock remained closed and undisturbed, while padding to the door and clasping the towel modestly around his waist.

"What do you want?"

"What . . . ! What d'you think I want, you lout."

Cautiously he pressed his ear against the door panel. He heard no creak of shuffling boots and no low breathing of men out in the hall with her.

Velvet said somewhat testily, "You going to let me deliver or make me keep yakking to myself?"

Fargo relented. Removing the chair from under the knob, he warily unlatched, then opened the door. Velvet slipped in. She leaned against the door, shutting it and relocking it with her hands behind her. She had changed from her dance-hall costume into a burgundy wrapper, and as she stepped toward Fargo, smiling, her figure stretched the garment, revealing intriguing curves and points of interest. She was not carrying anything. In fact, she appeared not to have come with anything, period, save her wrapper and a pair of ankle-length serge shoes.

Fargo said guardedly. "I'm not fit for visitors. What's the gag?"

"I gave you a kiss, you gave me a present. You also gave me a kiss, then, so now I must give you a present. It is our custom." She moved closer, letting her gown sweep back behind her, her eyes mocking. "I've only one thing of value, but I'm giving it freely, yours just for the taking."

Fargo was still suspicious. "Great. I'll unwrap it later."

"Oh, no, it's my gift to give." With an open mouth and slowly sliding tongue, she kissed him again, lazily, sensuously. "I'm no society-belle virgin, all coyness and tease," she murmured. "I'm rich man's baggage, remember? Fat Dan's honeypot, lately, and I willingly admit it."

"Bluntly, too."

"If there's anything this country does, it strips away the nonessentials." Laughing throatily, she shrugged off her wrapper.

Fargo couldn't help but smile. Velvet was a sensuous product, provocatively packaged. She looked up into his face and he could see that she seemed not only willing, but eagerly anticipating her gift-giving. She exuded sex, a blatant desire for it, and Fargo reacted lustily as her wrapper slid slowly to her feet, revealing her smooth, round breasts and the crescent between her tapering thighs. She raised her arms slightly to hold his shoulder with one hand and loosen his grip on the towel with the other. The towel almost hooked upon his growing erection, which she regarded delightedly.

"Oh, you're fit. Lordy, are you fit."

As she kicked off her shoes, Fargo braced the chair against the door again. He then threw his clothes off the bed and pulled her to him by the waist, lowering her onto the coverlet. He crawled in alongside her, kissing her breasts, suckling her nipples while his hands parted her sensitive loins, his fingers caressing, massaging as he eased his way inside.

Velvet sighed and mewed with growing arousal, her body undulating against him, her own hand slipping between them to rub and fondle him. "C'mon, sport," she panted, "Now, do it now . . ."

Fargo rose and knelt over her. She lay silent with anticipation, her legs spread on either side of him, her exposed pink furrow moist and throbbing. He levered downward, and she gasped with the rock-hard feel of him as he began his gentle entry. She pushed upward, her thighs clasping him, swallowing his full thick length up inside her.

"Lordy, lordy," she moaned, her muscles squeezing around with him so tightly that Fargo almost cried out the pleasure. He thrust, and she automatically responded in rhythm, mewing deep in her throat, her splayed thighs arching spasmodically against his pumping hips. Their pace increased, and increased again, their passion mounting greedily.

Soon their rhythm grew frenzied. She rolled him over, he rolled her over, back and forth, their nude bodies frantic in their pounding madness. Fargo's breath rasped in his throat; Velvet's legs cramped where they gripped his middle. There was nothing but exquisite sensation, no existence beyond the boundaries of their flesh.

Velvet squealed as her climax struck. Her nails raked Fargo's back with each spasm, her limbs jerking violently. Fargo felt his own swift orgasm, his juices spewing hotly into her. She absorbed all of his flowing passion, until, with a final convulsion, she lay still, satiated.

"Never with Fat Dan," she sighed blissfully. "Never like that." She stretched her legs back so she could lie with him inside her, and they dozed off, their bodies gently intertwined. . . .

Fargo awoke once to Velvet kissing him. Again they made love, savoring each fresh touch of their naked flesh, and afterward she cuddled against him while they sank back into lethargy, and Fargo drifted off to sleep again. . . .

He awoke a second time to a sharp *kersnap!* and a sudden yelp of a feminine voice. He sat up, hearing slightly muffled whimpers as though someone was crying through a mouthful of fingers. It was still dark, but he didn't know the time and really didn't care, intrigued by the dim outline of a naked young woman prancing with lively grace, removing her hand from her mouth, and waving it about while moaning and mewing and cussing like a sailor.

Fargo bust out laughing.

"What a rotten trick," she rebuked, stopping now and dipping her hand between her legs. "You should've warned me you had that sack booby-trapped."

"Mousetrapped, Velvet. To catch small rats."

"That's not fair! I worked hard to find where you hid it."

"You sure did. What're you going to tell Fat Dan?"

"I don't know. Something." She padded to the bed and flung the trap at Fargo. "Oh, you ruined everything. This was my big chance, and once I'd got it, I was going to vamoose on Fat Dan and everyone."

Fargo gave her a soft smile. "You can dress now."

Velvet hesitated for a moment, then climbed on the bed, her face screwed up into a little girl's pout. "Why do I have to? It's not morning yet, and I bet if we try, we can get something up before the sun . . . "

2

The day dawned crisp and blustery.

After breakfast at the rooming house, Fargo collected his Ovaro from the stable and left Glenns Ferry without further incident. As a precaution, though, he cut up a game path that flanked the Oregon Trail, the bouldered slope and wooded brush in between concealing him from view. He let the pinto set his own pace so Skye could remain more alert to his surroundings on the long, wearisome trek ahead.

Fargo nonetheless looked forward to reaching the Teton Basin. Old friends he hadn't seen for many months, even years, would be camping there at the infamous Pierre's Hole. For over half a century, trappers, hunters, and friendly Indians had gathered each summer to exchange news and lay in supplies, and from that had developed a similar encampment to serve for the winter months. In comfort and congenial company, mountain frontiersmen hurrawed away the cold weather while their shacks lay buried under the snow. Fargo did not intend to spend the season, but he did anticipate a good, well-deserved break.

But life is what happens when you make other plans.

Topping a ridge, Fargo scanned the broad, beaten

track below and saw a loose circle of wagons. Otis Wyndam's train, no doubt. It was comprised of eighteen high-tilted Conestogas and Pittsburghs all muddied and patched, their wheels with more rawhide binding on them than was right. He could spot women at cookfires and men tending cavvied oxen, but except for some children in homespun racing about, the camp lacked the usual noisy, boisterous air. That, he thought, might be due to the likes of Brigham Blutcher and the fact that today happened to be Sunday.

Turning his eyes eastward, Fargo glimpsed a lone wagon approaching along the trail about half a mile away. For a moment he sat asaddle, pondering the reason for it. There was little danger from Indians here, but still it was an unusual and foolish thing for a wagon to fall behind. He was about to move on when he spied three men, roughly midway between him and the oncoming Conestoga. They were crouched behind a rock upthrust, all packing revolvers, their carbines leaning against a rock behind them.

Fargo jigged forward till he was above the men. Ground-reining his Ovaro, he drew his Sharps and eased to the cover of a long spine of rock that angled up the ridge. It was, he judged, a holdup in the making, but he couldn't guess the reason for the one wagon lagging behind the others, nor the reason for the attack on this particular wagon.

It was a long wait. Fargo watched the men and built reloads for his Sharps, lining the extra charges on a flat stone beside him. Twice one of the men rose, had a quick look, and dropped back out of sight. He was short, thickset, and appeared to be the leader.

When the short man took his third look, the slow wagon had finally come abreast of them. Scooping up his carbine, he mounted, and when the others were in their saddles, he said something, then led the way out to the trail, setting a fast pace. Fargo laid his Sharps across the rock spine, hammer back, but he held fire until the trio reached the wagon. The short man held up his hand, the two behind him raising their carbines to cover the driver. Fargo had his sights on the short man, trigger finger tightening as he waited for the final proof that this was a holdup.

The wagon stopped. The driver and a woman stepped down from the seat. Without warning, one of the men fired. The driver doubled over, a hand clutching his chest. Then he spilled forward, the way a dead man falls, the woman dropping on her knees to his side.

Fargo shifted, catching the killer in his sights, and blasted him out of the saddle. Surprise caused the other two to wheel their horses, while the woman quick-wittedly pulled the pistol from the driver's holster. Fargo squeezed off another shot; a second man stiffened and reeled uncertainly before falling to the ground. The short man fired point-blank at the woman and missed in his haste. Her bullet plucked the hat from his head, making him jerk, which undoubtedly saved his life, Fargo's third shot skinning his arm. Panicking, the man whirled his mount away from the wagon and raced toward Glenns Ferry.

Fargo tore for the Ovaro, booted his Sharps, and remounted. His first impulse was to pursue, but he couldn't leave the woman alone with two outlaws who might not be dead. He plunged down the slope, cocked revolver in hand, and spurred for the wagon.

The woman was on her feet, ready to shoot him as another outlaw when he reined in. Hurriedly correcting her, Fargo checked the outlaws. One was dead. The other was unconscious, the bullet having cut a wicked furrow along his skull, but chances were he'd come to with little more than a headache.

Fargo turned back to the woman. He judged her to be about thirty, and though no ravishing beauty, she projected a presence that piqued his interest. She was dressed in worn, man-style range gear, except for a fancy blouse with a lot of needlework that accentuated her full-breasted, somewhat tall, and angular figure. Her features weren't perfectly regular, her nose being a bit long and her chin a bit clipped; yet from her low-crowned hat spilled luxuriant raven hair, which went well with eyes of deep onyx. At the moment they were wet and welling, yet filled with the kind of sorrow that would find no release in tears.

"Harold's dead." She pointed to the driver, who was so lanky he seemed all hide and bones. His hair and mustache were completely white. Age had marked his face with deep crossed lines, and now in death he seemed to be completely at peace.

"I'm sorry," Fargo said simply. "Your father?"

"My husband," she snapped, baring sharp, pearly teeth. Fargo got the idea she would like to sink them in his throat. "Why would they kill him?"

"What did they say when they rode up?"

"They told us to stop and get down. They said they wanted the money he'd hid in the wagon. Harold said he didn't have any. Then they shot him."

"Did you ever see those men before?"

"No."

"Well, the wounded one will be able to talk." Hearing riders, he glanced toward the wagon train and saw four horsemen galloping toward them. "Kind of slow, aren't they?"

"It wasn't their fault. We shouldn't have stayed behind, but Harold was sick. Had been since we left

28

Fort Hall. The dust made him cough, so we dropped back, and yesterday we had a minor breakdown that delayed us overnight."

Two of the riders were unknown to Fargo, but he recognized the flamboyant sombrero of Otis Wyndam and the parson's garb of Brigham Blutcher. As they reined up in front of the wagon, Wyndam called, "What happened, Miz Julia?"

While the woman told them, Wyndam and Blutcher looked at her dead husband with troubled sorrow. The man between them looked angry, and when Julia was through explaining, he turned on Wyndam, frowning.

"Otis, you had no business lettin' the Driscolls drop behind."

"Me! I'm not the train boss, I'm only guiding you to Oregon."

"Nor could it be helped," Blutcher snapped at the man. "We couldn't have waited and still reached this oasis by nightfall. You know we do not journey on the Sabbath."

"All I know is, Brimstone, Harold was the only real leader we had. Now we'll have a helluva time." Ignoring Blutcher's spluttering, the man scowled at Fargo. "What I don't know is who you are and what you're doin' here."

"The name's Skye Fargo." He jerked a hand toward the ridge. "I was up there when I saw these men, so I pitched in."

"I'm Roy Porter." The man dismounted and extended his hand. "You downed one an' wounded tuther, eh? Too bad you didn't save Harold's life."

Porter's implication couldn't have been plainer, and it rankled Fargo. He replied, "So am I," gave the hand a quick grip, and dropped it quicker. Porter was big, as tall as Fargo, and heavier. He had a flat nose, and his chin had the square jut of stubbornness, and his pale eyes brimmed with ambition. But his handshake made Fargo feel he'd been clutching the tail of a wet fish.

By then the fourth man had reined his horse behind Fargo. His pistol suddenly thundered, and Fargo, pivoting, drew his Colt.

"No trouble," Porter cried. "Turk just finished the gent you creased."

"He was pullin' a derringer out of his shirt," the man called Turk said. "If I hadn't just happened to see him, he'd have back-shot you, bub."

Hunkering by the outlaw, Fargo responded tightly. "He doesn't have a derringer or any kind of gun in his shirt or anywhere around him."

"Why, I swore he was shoving a hand inside his shirt when I drilled him," Turk said blandly. He was a two-gun man, rangy, with abnormally long fingers. His eyes, narrowed now as he watched Fargo, were as expressionless as those of a dead fish. Those eyes, Fargo thought as he stood, and Porter's hand should have been part of the same cadaver. In an injured tone, Turk added, "I reckoned I was saving your life, bub. You got a shabby way of thankin'."

"Fargo's spilled too much blood to be saved," Blutcher intoned.

"Blutcher, the Good Book says 'smite your enemies' or words to that effect," Fargo said in a low, chilled voice. "And I'm looking at the ass whose jawbone I'll be smitin if he doesn't shut up."

"Aw'ri', aw'ri'," Wyndam interjected, motioning wearily. "Let's not argue. C'mon, Brimstone, help me load poor Harold in his wagon. I've got to go to Glenns Ferry, but soon's I return, what say we hold a funeral."

"We'll send some men to bury this pair," Porter

said, tossing his reins to Turk. "I'll stick with Miz Julia till we pull into camp."

Julia Driscoll gave no response to this, but seemed to ignore Porter as she stepped over to Fargo, who was mounting his horse. "Thank you for what you did, Mr. Fargo. Please, won't you come to the service later?"

Fargo could tell little from the woman's set, frozen face. There was nothing to be gained by staying, and besides, it wasn't any of his business. But seeing Porter climb onto her wagon seat with obvious relish, and Blutcher glare at him with scowling disdain, gave Fargo sufficiently good reason.

"My pleasure, Mrs. Driscoll."

Out of courtesy, he and Wyndam waited trailside until the wagon was on its way to the camp. When they were alone, Wyndam said, "Lest you got something more pressing till the funeral, I'd not mind some company."

Shrugging, Fargo fell in alongside Wyndam and headed townward.

They jogged silently. When the buildings of Glenns Ferry loomed ahead, Wyndam said, "This whole thing has a smell about it that's bad. Apparently those men were waiting to get Harold." He cast Fargo a questioning glance. "Would a hundred dollars a week interest you?"

"No. Get one of the men on your train."

"They're farmers or tradesmen."

"Or self-annointed salvationers."

Wyndam chuckled. "Yeah, ol' Brimstone Blutcher can be an almighty pain sometimes. He's got a wife so tough a rattlesnake couldn't mark her hide, and a spunky daughter whom I'd strongly advise against harboring any fancy notions over. Truth be, I'd stay clear distance; Miracle can be poison honey. What

Brimstone doesn't have is gun skills or cold audacity in a crunch."

"Turk would fill that bill."

"I don't trust that man. He was admitted to the train only because of Roy Porter's recommendation."

"What about Porter?"

"I don't trust him, either," Wyndam muttered, and said nothing more until he reined in by Fat Dan's Grand Slam Casino. "I've got to talk to Tobin." He shifted uneasily. "I'm not real experienced at these things, Fargo. Will you go with me?"

Fargo said coldly, "I told you, I'm not a gun for hire."

Nodding, Wyndam dismounted and racked his horse. He was afraid. It was apparent in his twitching mouth, in the quick shifting of his eyes, but he walked into the casino anyway. Fargo watched him until the door shut behind him. Then conscience stirred within Fargo and he followed.

Wyndam was standing just inside the entrance, surveying the large room.

Fargo stepped around him and asked the bartender, "Where's the boss?" The bartender jerked a thumb toward the balcony. Fargo turned back to Wyndam. "Upstairs." He led the way, all the while thinking he was a damn fool, but what the hell.

Tobin's office was the first door, and Tobin was at his desk. He raised his head, saw who had come in, and dropped his gaze to the papers on his desk. As the door shut, he growled, "Folks generally knock before enterin'."

"We don't." Fargo crossed to Tobin. "Otis Wyndam's with a train east of town. I'm asking you to hear his speech, based on my personal recommendation."

Two spots of red appeared on Tobin's cheeks and spread across to the back of his neck as he recalled last night's events. He laid his pen down as Wyndam approached, tapped a bell on his desk, then regarded Wyndam with a deadpan expression. "What d'yuh want?"

"You to call off your thugs, that's what."

"Swell. Now what's that supposed to mean?"

"After we camped yesterday, six men came demanding a toll to ford the Snake. We saw 'em in Glenns Ferry later, me and another chap, when we went for supplies, and followed them into here. So don't act innocent with me."

A man, entering, strode over beside Tobin—a long-necked, bulging-browed man whose wide, swinging coat showed the butt of a low holstered revolver. He would be Fat Dan Tobin's trigger man, Fargo surmised, but Wyndam had failed to catch the significance of the man's entrance.

Tobin held his evenness of expression. "Yuh speak mean, pal."

"I plan to keep speakin' mean. We flat refuse to pay."

"Who's *we*? A decision by the train, or are yuh only speakin' for y'self?" Tobin sat back, tenting his fingers. "Does the toll come from their pockets or outta your hide, taken from your profits?"

"They'll buy my land when they get to it, which they can't if you rob them blind," Wyndam retorted, more boldly than Fargo had thought he'd speak. "We ain't payin' ten bucks a wagon, nor five per human or critter."

The long-necked man said, "The time to stomp snakes is when you first see 'em."

"Go ahead, Hank," Tobin said. "If anyone gets nosy, it's a holdup. Yuh hafta defend y'self when they hold yuh up, don't yuh?"

Watching the long-necked man, Fargo saw the lift

of his right shoulder. He went for his revolver the same instant the other's hand darted inside his coat. The two reports came virtually together, thunder-loud in the confines of the office and slamming in echoing reverberations against the walls. Twin tongues of flame lashed at each other across the desk. Lead breathed along Fargo's face. Then the gunman bent over, fingers gripping the corner of the desk. His pistol dropped from a relaxed hand as he lost his grip on the desk and fell, a loose lifeless body.

Tobin did not stir. He stared at Fargo's Colt which was lined on him now, smiling a little as he waved a soft hand, a gesture that said there was no more need of it. "Hank was fast, pal, faster'n Slick Dick. You outdrew him by half a second or he'd have got you."

"Maybe you'd like to give it a try?"

"No." Tobin shook his head. "I'd like you to work for me."

"I guess not." Retrieving Hank's pistol and disarming Tobin, Fargo backed toward the door. "We're leaving now."

Tobin rose. "Why're you working for this land shark?"

"I'm not. Just keeping him company."

Tobin glanced at the dead gunman as he settled back in his chair. "Pretty slippery company, pal, and you're a damn fool. He'll be gone soon, but I'll be set for a long time."

"Poke your nose out, and we'll see who gets to hell first."

The door key was in the inside latch. Fargo took it on their way out and locked the door from the balcony side, then pocketed the key as they went downstairs. They headed for the entrance, Wyndam a step ahead of him.

"Tobin meant to kill us, didn't he?" Wyndam said in a trembly voice. "Kill us in cold blood just like Harold Driscoll was killed."

"Yep. Say, you look like you could use a drink."

Wyndam stiffened. "I never imbibe alcoholic spirits."

"Well, I notice a thirst coming on," Fargo said at the entrance, and prodded Wyndam outside. "You go on. I'll catch up after I wet my whistle."

"Y'know, Fargo, you're in this fight now whether you like it or not." Wyndam paused, appraising the Trailsman, and added, "Unless you skedaddle."

"I'm staying for the funeral, remember?"

"Then you're a marked man. You might as well get paid."

"I'm not staying after the funeral, remember that too."

When Wyndam was gone, Fargo found an opening at the bar, ordered a whiskey, and stood with it between his fingers while he searched the place for the short man who'd survived Harold Driscoll's killing. If Fargo was reading the sign right, the outlaw would return home to roost. He glanced up at Tobin's office door, which soon began to quiver as though someone was wrenching and beating on it from the inside. Nary a sound of it carried, however, the casino crowded even at this early hour and filled with raucous noise.

It was ten minutes before Fargo picked his man out, standing alone at the other end of the mahogany. Fargo moved to stand beside him. He said softly, "I've seen you before."

The short man wheeled to face him. He was a little drunk, but not too drunk to be wary. He began backing away as he asked, "Who'n hell are you?"

"Skye Fargo. We've met, but I can't dab a loop on your handle."

"Tony Huff." The short man held his place, trying to recognize Fargo and failing. "I don't rec'lect you."

"Sure," Fargo said with grim certainty. "You ran with a couple of other gents who got shot this morning, while you were out killing Harold Driscoll."

Huff jerked, sloshing his beer. "You're tangling your spurs, mister. Must be some other guys you're thinking of."

"No, you're the jasper. I've been wondering who you work for, Huff. I could use you on a job."

"I don't work for nobody."

Huff was turning away from the bar when Fargo said, "Maybe I'll polish off the job I started, but I won't be doing it for blood money. I'm the one who plugged your buddies, Huff."

Huff's face went pasty white. He licked his lips, eyes involuntarily turning upward to the balcony. He had no stomach for a gunfight with Fargo, but fear of Fat Dan held him there. That was how Fargo read it, and he thought the man would break. He continued, "I'm giving you ten seconds, Huff. You want to talk or cash in your chips?"

"Huff, you scummy, suck-egg hound, pull your iron and turn a-smokin'!"

It was Turk's voice directly behind Huff. Huff wheeled, hand dropping to his gun butt, and he took Turk's bullet in his breastbone. He fell against the bar, eyes wide and unbelieving. He croaked, "Turk," and dropped then, sideways, and rolled over into a still, quiet heap.

Turk reholstered his pistol, mocking eyes on Fargo. "I think he aimed to kill you. You owe me your life twice. Quite a debt, ain't it, bub?"

"Quite a debt," Fargo allowed.

The crowd had fallen back with the first hint of

trouble. The bartender called, "Guess you had to do it, mister. I saw him reach first."

"Sure. I had to do it," Turk agreed. "I had trouble with him in Soda Springs last winter. He swore he'd plug me the first time we met."

A sense of failure beat at Fargo. He had been close to getting what he wanted, but not close enough. For the second time that day Turk's gun had silenced a man who might have talked. He glimpsed the bouncer heading up the stairs to notify Tobin, and figured it was time to make tracks, particularly considering he'd gain nothing more by sticking around. Pushing through the crowd into the street, he was unaware that Turk was following until he reached his horse and the gunman called to him.

"Whoa up, Fargo. You and me have got talk to make."

"Not with you."

"We're not fooling each other," Turk said. "I know a tough hand when I see one. If you're smart, we can wring this deal together."

"Then I guess I'm not as smart as you are. Me and Fan Dan wouldn't look good on the same side. You don't believe me, ask him in a couple of minutes."

"So you figure I'm playing close to Tobin."

"Aren't you?"

Turk ignored the question. He stood staring at Fargo, fingertips stroking his jaw thoughtfully. "What I'd like to know is how come you bit off a chunk of this. Tobin didn't pull you in. If Porter did, I'll kill him. You can tell him that."

Fargo stepped away from his horse. "If you're likewise bent on killing me, have at it."

Turk shook his head, his lips curving into a mocking grin. "I never rush jobs like this, Fargo. Before I beef you, I'll find out where you fit in this shindig.

Somebody's paying you, and I'd sure's hell like to know who."

As Turk turned away Fargo asked, "Did you come out here thinking I'd throw in with you?"

Turk chuckled. "No, but I thought you'd be mad enough to talk some. I made a mistake. You ain't that mad yet, but you will be when you see ten thousand dollars sliding out from under your nose. Then you'll talk 'cause you're smart enough to reckon that a part of ten grand is better'n nothing."

3

Harold Driscoll was buried that afternoon on a little knoll shaded by a few gnarled sycamores.

Julia Driscoll stood at graveside as if stunned, her face drained of color, her eyes moist. Roy Porter hovered beside her with an attitude of proprietorship, as though the new widow was already his woman. Turk was nearby, his cold eyes dulled, as if bored by the grief and good-byes. Other members of the wagon train were grouped about, their gazes often shifting covertly from the grave to Fargo. Obviously the tale of what had happened last night in Fat Dan's had spread through the camp, and it took no wild guess to know who had carried it. Brigham Blutcher. Annoyance prickled Fargo as he stood next to Wyndam, hat in hand, and listened to the aptly nicknamed Brimstone spout a eulogy while Driscoll was laid to rest.

One of the women put an arm around Julia and led her away, which seemed to vex Porter. He came over to Wyndam and said something about a council meeting, his wide-jawed face revealing a sullen anger at Fargo's presence.

Wyndam fished for a pipe and began filling it, waiting until Porter had stalked off with Turk before remarking wearily to Fargo, "Lord, I'm tired of trouble. I don't want any more."

"Tough. You've got it, ten thousand bucks of trouble."

The pipe almost dropped. "What?"

"As a guess, I figure it's how much all the settlers are carrying to pay for expenses and property."

Wyndam lit his pipe, eyes pinned on Fargo. He said reluctantly, "All right. A fair estimate, I hazard, but they're only carrying expenses. They wouldn't buy my land in advance, so I insisted those funds be collected and safe-kept in a strongbox."

"It's aboard the train?"

"Of course."

"Does everybody know where the box is?"

"No, nobody except me and Harold. After all, he was their train boss." Suspicion flickered suddenly in Wyndam. "You think that's got something to do with his killin'?"

"Fat Dan Tobin would go a long ways to get his grips on ten thousand," Fargo said bluntly. "And, no, don't ask. Running herd on a pile of money doesn't interest me, either. I'll be going now. I wish you well."

Fargo returned to the camp, where his Ovaro was tethered, and chanced to spot Julia Driscoll around back of her wagon. He walked over to say good-bye.

"I'm sorry you're leaving," Julia told him. "Saint or sinner, I believe Mr. Wyndam's correct in saying we need a man of your prowess."

"He told me you've had trouble. What kind?"

"Stock stampeded. Gunshots at night. In the morning we'd find bullet holes in the wagon tops. Little things that've kept the train worked up."

"And sore at your husband?"

"My, yes. Harold was elected leader as a compromise between Porter and Blutcher. He shouldn't have accepted, he simply wasn't well enough, particularly for the abuse they all heaped on him."

There was a moment of silence, Julia waiting for Fargo to give her reasons for his questions. But Fargo was considering the pattern that was shaping up in his mind—a web of scheming, greed, and murder. Then, seeing that no explanation was forthcoming, Julie continued, "Harold thought it was his duty, though. When he was alive, he balanced things up. Now there's Porter's bunch and Blutcher's bunch, and the council's split like it was at the beginning."

"Julie." It was Roy Porter's voice.

Sighing, she called, "What is it, Roy?"

Porter saw Fargo then, and rage flowed into him. He came toward the tailgate, hands fisted, head shoved forward on his shoulders. "If you got anything to say to Miz Julia, do it where people can see you."

"Maybe you're watching out for her interests?" Fargo asked softly.

"I sure as hell am," Porter snapped. "Somebody's got to, now that her husband's dead."

Julia broke in, "Mr. Fargo was not bothering me."

Porter ignored her, confronting Fargo. "I sure as hell won't put up with no gunslick wolfer taking her behind the wagon and wooin' her up and—"

Fargo hit him then, a short right to Porter's jaw that snapped his head back. Porter bellowed a curse and drove at Fargo, fists hammering the air in their frantic urge to reach Fargo's face. Fargo dropped to his hands and knees, and Porter, rushing wildly, stumbled over him and fell hard, facedown.

Fargo rose rapidly to his feet and dropped on Porter, knees in the man's ribs. He heard the crunch of bones, the hiss of suddenly expelled breath. He jerked Porter's hat from his head and threw it aside.

Then, with a fistful of Porter's hair, he raised the man's head and brought it down hard, burying his nose in the dust. And again, then again, battering and grinding.

Julia was begging for them to stop. Others were coming and ganging around, the crowd growing, Wyndam calling for order. Anger ran through Fargo, hard brutal anger that touched his blood with fire. He felt Porter go slack, heard him yowl, "I'm done! I'm done!" Fargo rose, watching for the first hostile move as Porter struggled upright and glared at him, a hand feeling his bruised jaw.

"I won't forget this, Fargo," Porter snarled.

"Don't. You got the body of a bull but the brains of a rabbit," Fargo said scornfully. "Remember that the next time you feel like talking tough."

Instead of Porter replying, a woman in the crowd berated Fargo with a ripsawing voice: "A born gentleman ain't no match for a ruffian like you, a coursehanded hellion who'd always take brutal advantage over his fellow man."

Pivoting, Fargo saw the woman and knew right then and there she was Mrs. Blutcher. For one thing, she was standing beside Brimstone, and for another, she was formidable. A corpulent, middle-aged woman with graying hair swept back tightly into a bun, she had big ox eyes the color of old chocolate, an anvil for a chin, and the biceps and thighs of a circus strongman.

Brimstone was nodding smugly, and apparently Mrs. Blutcher also carried weight with the crowd, for many of them were adding grunts and nods of agreement. Not one to leave such an opportunity undone, Porter pointed a finger at Fargo and snapped, "You were there when Harold was killed. Now you're here cozying his grief-stricken widder an' knockin' me

42

lips. "You'll never come back. Either you'll wind up in Tobin's boothill or you'll keep riding."

Fargo turned from the others. Wyndam and then Julia fell into step with him as he strode to his horse, Wyndam saying, "You shouldn't have let that ol' she-blister rile you, Skye. Her tongue's as long as a fence rail, I swear."

"Never mind. Whatever you do, keep Turk here. I'll probably be late, because I won't be able to pull this off till after dark, so build up a fire that'll give us good shooting light by the time I get back." He smiled softly then at Julia. "I need to borrow a horse and gear."

"Harold's roan saddler." She led him to the cavvy, then back to her wagon for the gear, but she did so reticently. When finally Fargo led the roan over to his Ovaro, Julia gripped his arms. "Don't go. I don't care about the horse, I give it freely, but this isn't your fight, Skye—Mr. Fargo."

"Skye." Mounting, he swung his horse around and stared down at her. "I'll see what I can do about staying alive," he told her, and with roan following, reins tied to his saddle, he headed toward Glenns Ferry.

Shortly he turned south from the trail and climbed the flanking slope to the game trail he'd ridden that morning. There he waited, eyes on the yonder camp, while the sun dropped behind the Rockies and twilight flowed across the Snake River plateau. Dusk became night. Campfires were red jewels forming a round frame, and toward the west, lamps in Glenns Ferry flickered in the darkness to mark Fat Dan Tobin's town.

It was not until full night had come that Fargo remounted and rode into Glenns Ferry. To walk boldly into the Grand Slam Casino was the surest way of getting his hands on Tobin. To bring him out the same was certain failure and suicide. There had to be another avenue of escape, but it would be a ticklish job at best. Turk may've been right when he said anybody trying it would get nothing but a dose of lead poisoning.

Fargo left the horses in the deep shadows at the edge of town and slowly circled the casino building. An emporium stood next door. Its roof was not steep-sloped. A man dropping to it from one of the upper windows of the casino would risk nothing more than a jarring fall, but keeping a prisoner was another question.

Studying the hotel roof now in the yellow light flowing from the row of windows along the casino's balcony, Fargo saw that it was far from good, but it would have to do. The two end windows would be in Tobin's office. The next two were lighted, the third dark. That, he realized, would be the room that would furnish his avenue of escape with Fat Dan.

Fargo swung into the street and stepped through the entrance. He gave a quick glance around the crowded room, eyes probing the smoke-blued air, and saw neither Tobin nor Turk. He could reasonably count on Wyndam holding Turk, especially with the aid of Porter's rival, Brimstone. If Wyndam did the job, Tobin would not be forewarned, and in surprise lay the best chance of success.

Fargo went up the stairs and into Tobin's office. Closing the door, he s,tood against it, revolver fisted. Tobin was at a window, a drink in his hand, eyes on the street. Without turning, he asked, "Any news from Turk?"

"No news, Fat Dan," Fargo said softly. "Turk's not leaving camp."

Tobin whirled, eyes pellets of ice. "Pushing your luck, ain't you?"

"I always push it." Fargo heard steps on the balcony and pressed against the wall. The houseman, Proust, came in, and as he cleared the doorway, Fargo's revolver looped down across his head. He caught the falling body and eased him to the floor. Toeing the door shut, he said, "If Proust saw me, might be someone else did, too. That leaves me short of time."

"Now that you're in, you wish you weren't," Tobin taunted.

"No. It's fine so far. I came after you."

Tobin's laugh was forced. "No man alive can be as tough as you set yourself up to be. You'll never get me down the stairs, pal."

"Then we'll go another way. All I want you to do is go to the wagon camp and talk to them. Hell, I'll even give you your gun back when we get there."

"I'll never come back alive."

"You will if you behave. They've some ideas about law." Fargo motioned toward the door. "Get moving."

The expressionless mask was on Tobin's face again. "The only way out is down the stairs. You'll be in hell before you get to the bottom."

Fargo waited until Tobin was at the door. He patted him down, found a replacement hideout gun for the one he'd taken earlier, then turned Tobin away from the stairs, his gun muzzle digging him in the back. "Keep to the wall. Go through the third door."

"What the hell . . ."

"Quiet. I want to get you to the camp alive. And I don't aim to die myself."

Tobin kept his silence until they were in the room. Then he asked, "Where does this get you?"

"We're going through the window. We'll drop to the roof and hit the ground off the southeast corner."

Tobin looked down from the window. Fargo felt a shudder pass through him, Tobin shrinking back. "I could bust a leg . . ."

"Hang by your hands and bounce."

As if seeing a chance to escape, Tobin let himself through the window, moving fast, drooped, and started to run. He slipped and sprawled headlong.

Close behind him, Fargo said, "I'll drill you if you make a run, Fat Dan."

Fargo was never certain what Tobin had in mind. Carried by the impetus of his fall, he started to roll. He attempted to bring himself to his hands and knees, but couldn't achieve it in time. He reached the edge of the roof, clawed frantically for a hand-hold, and failed to get it. He went off, falling hard into a pile of rubbish, breath knocked out of him.

Fargo dropped alongside. "It's a good thing for you that you didn't make that try good."

Tobin lay staring at him, lacking even the breath to curse. Fargo pulled him upright and propelled him through the blackness, gun muzzle hard against his back. Five minutes later they had mounted the horses and left the lights of Glenns Ferry behind.

"I've got nothing to talk to these sodbusters about," Tobin complained. "All I need is time and it'll all fall into my hands like a ripe plum."

"Now that Harold Driscoll is dead."

Tobin jerked. "You add better than I thought."

"And if Turk keeps at his job of kicking at trouble, and Porter gets elected as the next train boss."

"You know about them too?" Surprise deepened on Tobin's face, but he hastily recovered. "Well, it don't make no difference. Enjoy it while you can, pal, 'cause it ain't going to last long."

Tobin dropped into sullen silence and presently they reached the camp. Fargo skirted the circle until he came to the Driscoll wagon, then reined around it and rode into the firelight, the eyes of the surprised settlers rising to meet them.

Wyndam let out a laugh. "Hell's teeth, he got Tobin!"

Fargo dismounted, Tobin following, and the Trailsman handed him back his pistol. He said, "Fat Dan had some ideas about getting back. I promised him he'd have back his own iron."

"About like handing a rattlesnake's poison back to him," Brimstone griped. "What kind of deal with him do you expect to make, Fargo?"

"That's for you to figure out. Tell me, though, has Porter ever said he'd been around these parts before?"

Porter began, "I won't stand—"

"Shut up!" Fargo nodded at Brimstone and Wyndam. "Has he?"

"Yeah, he mentioned he'd been here an' all over the West, scouting for a place to homestead," Wyndam answered. "He joined the train 'cause he'd decided on Oregon."

"And you said Turk joined on Porter's say-so, right?" Fargo took a pace away from the fire so he could watch Porter and Turk, who stood together across the blaze from him and Tobin. "We've got the pieces now if we can put them together. Porter must've told Tobin about the money aboard the train. Maybe to pay a gambling debt, maybe just to rig a deal. Tobin got him to put one of his tough hands in with you. That right, Porter?"

"Lies," Porter said between clenched teeth. He stared around the circle of faces. "You're lying," he insisted vehemently.

Fargo grinned. "You've some friends in this group,

Porter. You wanted to be voted boss, so you'd be privy to where the strongbox was hidden. Since Driscoll was elected, you've done your damnedest to turn folks against him. The funny part about it is that even Mrs. Driscoll, who's got cause enough to see you dead, is a better friend of yours than Turk or Fat Dan Tobin."

Turk's cold eyes were on Porter. "You believe the bastard, Roy?"

"Today Turk told me that if you'd brought me into this ruckus," Fargo said sharply, "he'd kill you. That sound like a good friend, Porter?"

Porter stepped away from Turk, eyes darting from Fargo to Turk and back to Fargo. He licked his lips, the corners of his mouth twitching.

"Don't loose your head, Porter," Tobin warned.

"Tobin asked Wyndam if the toll would come from everyone or from his profits," Fargo went on, "which means he knew who Wyndam was, what he does. How'd he know that if he didn't hear it from you, Porter?" Fargo paused, waiting for the settlers to catch the full significance of this. Then he said bluntly, "You can talk now, Porter, and maybe undo some of the cussedness you've had a hand in."

"I thought you brought me here to talk business," Tobin interjected, eyes flashing angrily.

"We'll talk business when we put our cards on the table," Fargo snapped. "Porter, you'd better face those cards. If you keep playing with Fat Dan, you'll wind up with a slug just like Harold Driscoll did. Or the outlaw I wounded, or Tony Huff in the casino. That's the way Tobin plays, Porter. Your only chance to live is to talk. You're a dead man if you don't because when this is over, you won't be any use to Fat Dan."

"All right!" Porter cried in a frantic rush. "You've got it figured—"

"Damn you!" Turk made a fast draw.

Porter yelled, "No! No!" Then his words were lost in the thunder of several guns.

Fargo's draw matched Turk's, but he wasn't quick enough to keep Porter from being shot. Turk's bullet slammed into Porter and spun him staggering toward Turk, momentarily blocking Fargo's line of fire.

Fargo sprang to one side, lead searing the air where he had just been, and a swift glance showed him it had come from Fat Dan Tobin. He swiveled in a low crouch and returned fire, his hasty shot missing vitals but flicking Tobin's inner shirt sleeve near his armpit, sufficient to send the fat man plunging in a roll under a shielding wagon.

"Git 'way," Turk was shouting at Porter, and fired again and once again hit Porter. In shocked agony, Porter blundered on, the force of his sagging body driving Turk backward. Soggily he fell, pinning Turk to the ground.

Fargo was using the instant to concentrate on Tobin, who was firing as he dragged himself deeper under the wagon. Then lead from Fargo's Colt shattered the bone in his thigh, its impact tugging a moan from him and slamming his face into the dirt. He started raising himself, triggering desperately, the slug from his wavering pistol coming amazingly close by chance, burning a groove in the knee of Fargo's pants. An answering bullet drilled him in his heart, and Tobin collapsed without another sound.

A bullet clipped Fargo's hat. He whirled to face Turk, who had shoved Porter off and was now in a sitting position and aiming his revolver to shoot again. The slug that Fargo bored into Turk's breastbone slammed him back flat on the ground. He writhed weakly there, mouth gasping, eyes bulging, fingers scratching at the dirt. He still held on to his .44, however, and as Fargo triggered again, Turk managed to snap off a shot that whistled past his cheek, its breath hot and vicious.

Then all grew very still.

Hurrying to Porter, Fargo swung his arm at the settlers who'd ducked for cover. "Thanks for backing me, you pack of gutless cowards," he raged, hunkering.

Porter gave a coughing moan, but he was dead and just didn't know it. Then, shuddering, he relaxed to sprawl inert.

They came back into the circle of light, shamefaced. Wyndam said, "Guess we can't do no braggin', but at least we got Porter sized up right now. Likewise Turk. Foxes in our henhouse, pure and simple, out after our money. Is that what lay behind Harold being held up and shot?"

"Yeah. I guess Tobin reckoned he couldn't lose. Either Driscoll told where your money was hidden, or he didn't and Porter would be elected—"

"O'er my dead body," Brimstone roared.

"Likely," Fargo drawled. "Another ploy to learn the location of your strongbox was demanding a toll. Porter and Turk were here on hand to see where Driscoll or you, Wyndam, went to get the money to pay it."

"How'd you know Turk would go for his gun? Or Porter would fess up?"

"Men of that caliber act about the same. I'd seen Turk shoot two men to keep them from talking, so I figured he'd pull the same stunt if Porter broke. To rope Tobin in, I had to risk giving him his gun to fight with."

"Porter?"

"No sand in his craw. I found out he was just a lot

of words when we had that tussle. It was a case of piling it on till he cracked from the strain."

Nodding, Wyndam took off his fancy hat and said, "We're beholden to you, Skye. You can see how much we need you to join us."

"Hell, no," Fargo said quickly. "I don't want any part of your crazy caravan."

Brimstone and his wife made satisfied grunts, blatantly dead set against Fargo continuing on with the train. Fargo also detected a gleam of hellfire in Wyndam's oh-so-humble eyes; again he wondered about this land speculator. He found no answer, but it caused him to wonder how these worried, haggard settlers would endure the privations and perils of the Oregon Trail, and if their dream of the Promised Land would become a disastrous, doom-laden nightmare.

Then Julia Driscoll smiled and batted her eyelashes and asked invitingly, "At least stay for dinner with me, won't you?"

"Well . . ."

4

"Catch up! Catch up!"

For five days now that cry had awakened Skye
Fargo at dawn. Five days, fifty miles, always on to
the west. They'd come through rivers that tightened
the squeaks out of the wagons, and across rugged
hills that brought the squeaks back with more beside,
and Oregon seemed no nearer. The Cascade Range
was still a blue barrier barring the western horizon,
but the harsh Snake River plains were very real
about them.

Not surprisingly, Brimstone Blutcher had been
elected train boss, and not surprisingly, he lorded it
over everyone. Fargo was content to leave such mat-
ters to the settlers. He made a point to stay away
from the wagons between dawn and dusk, acting as
wing scout and hunting fresh game.

Of course, that gave him little time to see Julia
Driscoll—she who had persuaded him to remain with
the train; or rather, who had sabotaged his plans to
leave with warm smiles and a superb pot-roast dinner. She continued to flash him promising smiles
and lingering glances, yet she was, after all, a new
widow, with her late husband barely cold in the
ground, and was no round-heel pushover to boot.
And as for the evenings, messing around was difficult if not impossible. After the night meal, the set-

tlers gathered for group singing—what Blutcher called jolly Singspirationals and Fargo called stockyard caterwauling. Then they'd retire to their wagons, save for a rotating picket of night guards.

As far as Fargo was concerned, the only thing good about these singalongs was Pickadilly Ike. Grizzled, rheumy-eyed, with few teeth and fewer hairs, Pickadilly Ike was a cantankerous coot who'd once scouted for Bridger and been a pard of Carson's, or so he bragged. He fibbed outrageously, gargled shellac, and pissed vinegar, but whenever he brought out his homemade banjo to pick and sing, he always drew a rapt audience.

Pickadilly Ike drove a canvas-topped Murphy freighter, about half the size and weight of the other wagons. That was all the home he needed, for those who pioneered the wild frontiers learned to travel light. It was a lesson some of the settlers had yet to be taught. The Rasmussen family, for example, was hauling a Bilhorn "Happy Home" parlor organ. Even dumber, hooked onto the tailgate of the Blutcher Conestoga was Abigail Blutcher's prized two-wheel Acme dog cart, which on occasion she would rig to a pony and go a-ridin' in society style.

That dog cart wound up both a boon and a bane to Fargo.

The boon came second evening out, when Fargo purposely returned late to miss the singalong. Brimstone and Abigail Blutcher were leading the group howl, but the Blutcher daughter was back at their wagon. Miracle Blutcher had a gamine face, with freckles and blue eyes and a pert snub nose, and straight hair the color of new pine shavings. She wore a wash-faded daisy print dress that had stubby sleeves and five big yellow buttons running from the collarless neck to her waistline, and she wore it the way a grape wears its skin. She couldn't have been more than twenty or more than five feet tall, but she was still a woman to think of as a woman. A man could really fiddle with such imaginings, if he were fool enough to disregard Wyndam's dire warning.

Miracle was just trying to climb out the rear end of the wagon when Fargo rode up. The dog cart was in her way, and more than once Fargo had heard Abigail Blutcher yell she'd flay alive anyone who dared to touch it, but in trying to avoid the cart, Miracle snagged her dress on the short stub of the stout end of the coupling pole. She was caught there, high and astride of the gate, the left side of her dress skirt ripped almost to the waist. Fargo was just in time to swing in close and slip a quick forearm under her knee to help her on over, then very gently he eased her down to the ground.

Miracle smiled, saying, "Thanks. Only now I have to crawl back in again an' change." She started hoisting herself up over the tailgate, not the least bit embarrassed by her display of firm, pert, naked buttocks. "I had to come get a songbook, an' who-ee, I'll be in for it now. You best git, too. She catches us like this, she'll lay you flat out with her tongue. Why Pa ever let hisself be talked into marryin' Abigail after my ma died is more'n I can tell."

"In other words," Fargo said, "you and your dad aren't afraid of her, you're just cautious."

Miracle laughed and closed the canvas flap.

Poison honey, Fargo thought as he moved on; how sweet it is . . .

The bane happened on the fifth night. It was as a consequence of the night before, the fourth, and led to serious repercussions a week later.

On the fourth night, Abigail Blutcher swept Fargo aside and accused, "I know you're foxin' around, sparkin' dear li'l Miracle."

"No, I—"

"What real, worldly men like you can see in these empty-headed girls is beyond me. She'll be fifty years old before she has a lick of sense. I'm just thirty-three. If I'd had more sense at the time, I wouldn't have married Brigham Blutcher when I was seventeen, but even then I had more sense than Miracle will have at forty."

"Wait a minute, y'mean you—"

"Even smart men can be slow and stupid when it comes to a woman, Skye Fargo. Tomorrow night I'll have things ready for *us*, if I have to burst a skillet filled with hot grease over Brigham's thick skull." She seemed to sense his shock and aversion, tweaking his cheek coyly between thumb and forefinger. "Why, what an odd look you have in your eyes. What's the matter? I'm not going to eat you."

Abigail didn't add the word they both were thinking: *yet*

The incident was unnerving and so unexpected that Fargo reckoned he must've misinterpreted her advances. Abigail Blutcher enjoyed seeing the worst of everything and had disliked him from the start. Still, such women sometimes found that sort of thing perversely exciting. Fargo kept a wary eye out and himself well gone the following day, wondering what he could do if she did make a play. He couldn't shoot her. He might shoot himself.

That fifth evening they circled the wagons on a field bordering the Boise River. The stock cavvy was pastured off to one side, where the field sloped down to a marshy patch of tules and swamp grasses, and Fargo decided he was safer spreading his bedroll with the animals there than with the settlers. Moreover, it was after dark and the singing was done when he arrived back at camp.

He didn't take note of the dog cart until it was too late.

He was searching the murky acreage, straining to catch the slightest noise, when he heard a creak, the simpering of a giggle. He stiffened. "Who's there?"

"Surprise! Li'l me." Abigail rose from the bed of her dog cart, which was parked on the bank as though left after an earlier ride. One hand was daintily lifting a wrapper of gigantic folds, a Bedouin tent with a belt like a boa constrictor enwrapping her waist. "I thought you may prefer to meet here, away from interruptions, you sly devil, you."

"Jesus." Fargo was stunned motionless as she stood balancing in her cart, unbelting her wrapper. Widening the gown, she exposed a swath of pale flesh, then gradually let it slide down kettle breasts and a caldron belly, over hips of hamhock and legs of mutton, off to puddle around her feet. She leaned toward him, legs spread wide, Amazonian thicket poised, the cart wavering.

"Have me," she whispered.

"A misunderstan—"

"You probably think you prefer those skinny girls with lemon breasts and ribs you can count at a distance. Good only for making bruises, believe me." Her hand uncoiled, doing a pantomime of milking in the night air. "You won't be sorry. I'll show you a little specialty that made me famous all the way to Chicago."

"You can't be serious."

"I am, dearie." Pirouetting, she gazed about. "Where? Not on the ground; too dirty and hard. What about—*oh!*"

In turning, Abigail had set the cart to teetering. She tried to regain the balance, overcompensated, and the cart tongue reared into the air. The cart's load abruptly shifting, her great naked bulk dumped backward and jarred the wheels free of their chocks.

Fargo stared disbelievingly as the cart began rolling downhill. Abigail scrambled frantically to stop it, squawling, but the cart trundled on, picking up speed. He watched it jouncing toward the river, Abigail tossing her head, her vast coral mouth agape, wailing with increasing incoherency. The camp was awakening. A shout arose, immediately swelling to a chorus of alarm.

The cart hit a strip of gravel toward the bottom, then boulders. The cart tongue rammed between the rocks, slamming it to a halt, catapulting Abigail out in a low sailing arc. Her flustered scream was a brief yet moving cry that choked off abruptly in a massive, soggy splat. The cart splintered into kindling, while years of undisturbed mud suddenly fountained up from the marsh bed and rained sifting down on the tules.

The settlers dashed to rescue Abigail.

Fargo made himself scarce.

He never did learn what excuse she used to explain the situation, nor did he ask, merely content that from then on, Mrs. Blutcher kept a chilly distance. He was aware that her spurned seduction now seethed in the thick jungle of her loins with vindictive appetite.

The next day the wagon train reached Fort Boise. The fur-trading post was small, its palisade walls no more than a hundred yards long on each side. Behind the post, a small settlement bloomed, rowdy with trappers, prospectors, mountain men, and the riffraff who preyed on them. There was also a band of ragtag Indians who soon visited the wagon camp, willing to work like mules for scraps of food and clothing.

The train laid over an additional day, the Sabbath, which proved to be no blessing. Along about midafternoon, Brimstone returned from the post with two strangers, and announced, "Brethren, these fine fellows, Cheney Rutherford and Gus Logan, are addin' their wagon. Struck the deal during lunch t'day. They've had a run of bad luck and need the extra protection our train can give them."

Cheney Rutherford was a handsome, slick-dressing dude, his hair flaxen yellow and his eyes amber-colored, with a kind of film over them. But Fargo didn't care for the shape of his mouth; the lips were too thin, and the mouth was turned down at the corners. Rutherford's companion, Gus Logan, was powerfully built and pug-ugly, bigger than Fargo, with slouching stride and abnormally long arms ending in great, gnarled hands. His mane of auburn hair hung down to the collar of his mackinaw, which he wore with a wool shirt, stagged trousers, and low-heel calked boots. Both men were armed, their cartridge belts and revolvers appearing well-used yet well-maintained.

Otis Wyndam did not cotton to the pair either, commenting later to Fargo, "I'm loath to take 'em along, but I suppose the law of the trail leaves us no choice. Well, leastwise their guns will be handy if the Indians attack."

Most of the settlers, though, welcomed them without question. Indeed, as the train again moved onward, Cheney Rutherford and Gus Logan began to be looked upon as most helpful gentlemen, for they were constantly on the go from one wagon to another, politely suggesting and showing how this or that should be done. The ladies especially liked Rutherford, who'd agree and tip his hat every ten seconds or jump to his feet like a stiff-legged cook when any female came within forty feet of him. Logan thumped two husbands who took issue with Rutherford's smarm, but he lost no favor; Gus was not bad-hearted, merely a natural bully boy, a quick man with a blow.

Initially Fargo had no trouble with them. He rarely saw them during the day, and at night they held court with the Blutchers. "To say nothing of an odor about those two," Pickadilly Ike remarked to Fargo, "that keeps a gent with a sensitive nose shyin' away."

Pickadilly Ike didn't worry about them, however, finding the weather more aggravating and the Indians more threatening. Ever since they left Fort Boise, it had been raining a cold, soaking drizzle. The farther they rolled along the forty-five miles to the Oregon border, the heavier grew the showers, the thicker drew the cloud veil, and the worse it affected Pickadilly Ike's rheumatism. Fortunately he'd packed along a large supply of Dr. Seigismund's Magnetic Oil Tonic, guaranteed to ease pain of neuralgia, sciatica, lumbago, toothache, chilblains, and childbirth. Fargo could well believe it after one tentative sip; the patent medicine must've been a hundred and fifty proof.

Pickadilly Ike's tonic was also good for nerves, and Indians got on his something fierce. It was probably a leftover reaction from his fighting youth, for the Indians following the train were, by all appearances, a harmless scavenger band of thirty old bucks and squaws. As Rutherford scoffed at one evening's songfest, "It's no strange, scary bugaboo, such parties of old and broken reds drifting on the beg."

"Injuns ain't born for that kind of thing," Pickadilly Ike retorted. "For thousands of years they've been hunters an' warriors. Age an' hunger won't change their blood habits."

Rutherford laughed at him. "You could whip any two with one hand."

"I'd use both, and feet and guns if they cotched me! But I'm sayin' now, Ruddyfor', they'd sure have a footrace on their hands."

By the next morning the clouds were a sooty blanket hooding the sky, and the rains were a stormy downpour drenching Indian and settler alike. The wagons began having serious problems, sliding and sinking in deepening gumbo.

Brimstone goaded everybody on, refusing to help or delay the train when anyone became stuck. "Move! Don't stop," he commanded from horseback, riding up and down while his wife drove their wagon. The settlers obeyed, cursing, shoving, amid pistol cracks of bullwhips.

Fargo decided he'd do the most good by scouting immediately ahead of the wagons for soft stretches to avoid. Presently he came upon a bare patch of ground that looked like merely a stretch of damp sand, but his experienced eye noticed the little rim of saw grass. Returning to the first wagon, he advised Otis Wyndam to shun the spot. From the seat of the second wagon, Abigail Blutcher cast him a curdling glare and drove ahead, because, not in spite, of his warning.

The long and heavy Blutcher wagon bogged quickly, little bubbles of water coming up around the wheels as it settled buried to the bed. Abigail sat helpless on the front seat, the three yokes of oxen standing out of danger on hard ground while Brimstone galloped here and there, trying to coax other settlers to unhook teams for their wagons and help pull him free. He saw Fargo and Wyndam, but for some reason he came spurring on past Wyndam as if he had not seen him and swung in beside Fargo.

"I've got to have some help," Brimstone shouted.

"Help mightn't help as much as you hope." Fargo

reined up and studied the bogged wagon. "You've been worrying the devil out of your oxen, and oxen can't stand worrying and hurrying like teams of mules or horses. They'll drop in their tracks and die on you. So first you'll have to empty your wagon—"

"*Unload!*" Brimstone's eyes bugged. "Scatter my belongings on the ground in this weather?"

"Afraid so. Unload, knock loose your bolster stakes, and snake the bed off, then you can cut your coupling pole and pry out the running gear a piece at a time. It's the only way I see for you to get unstuck."

"You're mad! Double- or triple-teaming will haul it loose."

"I doubt it." Fargo flicked the reins and his Ovaro began walking on. "They're apt to break out your tongue and make a worse mess of it."

"Danged little I might've expected of you!" Brimstone wheeled away.

Fargo was busy for a spell after that, but shortly he glanced back to where Blutcher's wagon still sat in the bog hole, now with Rutherford and Logan and a few other men gathered around. He could see Brimstone no longer waving his hands and dictating orders, but standing rather dejectedly to one side until he turned and looked ahead at Fargo. He then shook his fist, seeming to dance a few steps of a jig. Fargo, chuckling, resumed his ride.

When finally the settlers circled that evening, they hovered in the wind-lashing rain, shivering at the prospect of a cold night. The Blutchers came late, last in line rather than up at the head, and a singalong was not even suggested. Instead, Brimstone slogged through the dismal camp carrying a coiled bullwhip, features congealing with rage as he approached Fargo.

"You're goin'! T'night, Mr. Fargo, on your way!" He leaned forward, eyes aflame. "We cannot tolerate your underminin' authority, flaunting contempt, inciting anarchy. Mount your horse and be gone unless—unless," he was getting out the rest of it in gasps, "you're prepared to fight."

"Brimstone, you're bloating too damned fat for your britches," Fargo replied sharply. "It was you who spouted the rule of no aid for one another, but being a sanctimonious hypocrite, soon as you got caught—"

"You call me—you call me that!" Brimstone looked as if he were suddenly going to froth at the mouth. "You—you cheap cutthroat and rake, I'll—"

And that was as far as he threatened, sputtering the rest as he slung the whip unwinding behind his head. It slashed forward then, the long end of it winding and slapping a good eight feet of it around Fargo. It hurt like bloody bejeezus, but Fargo had enough padding, what with his clothes and oilskin slicker, to withstand the excruciating pain. And infuriated, he grabbed hold of the whip and gave it a ferocious yank, snatching the whip handle out of Brimstone's clutch and Brimstone clear off his feet.

Brimstone stumbled forward, chin outstretched. Fargo fisted it smack on the button, and Brimstone caromed against the sideboard of Pickadilly Ike's wagon so hard that splintering could be heard. He dropped, momentarily stunned breathless. Grinning, Fargo tossed the whip aside. He glimpsed Wyndam hastening to them, face long and fretful. Rutherford and Logan, among others, were also converging. Fargo gestured at the two men and started to say, "Well, well, the coyotes come to the carcass—"

Brimstone was rising to his feet, and he rose punching.

"So go greet them," Fargo finished, seizing Brimstone by the wrist. He swung himself about, seemed to go down rolling on his back as though Brimstone had successfully charged him, his right foot kicking up. Brimstone spread out, eagle-winged, flying through the air. Fargo booted him in the belly, loosening his grip on the wrist.

Brimstone turned over in the air, still flying like a giant bird. Awkwardly he plowed into Rutherford and Gus Logan, so that the whole crew of them tangled and collapsed, all disarranged on the sloppy ground, Brimstone floundering among them. Unpious curses rent the air.

The men of the camp were closing around, Wyndam's voice calling for order. Rutherford extricated himself bellowing, his shiny boots, trimmed hair, and wondrously clean linsey and shirt now totally coated with gooey mud. Logan was similarly plastered, but didn't seem to mind that, intent on drawing his bowie knife and slitting Fargo's gizzard.

Fargo stood, knees bent, and laughed. "Why, it was only an Irish wrestling trick. We were only joking, and I showed him how it's done."

Rutherford came on, glowering, growling threats. Gus Logan was gliding in for a knife stroke. From behind Fargo a voice drawled, "The gent's right! Just a joke. A good one . . . on Brimstone."

Rutherford stopped coming. Logan froze in his tracks. The others hesitated, perplexed and thoughtful. Fargo turned and grinned at Pickadilly Ike, who sat on the tailgate of his wagon, a sawed-off blunderbuss across his knees. The weapon was as devastating as a cannon filled with grapeshot at that short range. It was carelessly aimed at Rutherford and Logan, Pickadilly Ike's fingers idly stroking the trigger.

Brimstone, pale, glittering with hatred, regained his feet. He said to the settlers, "Just a trick he showed me, uh-huh. It shan't happen again, I assure you."

Logan snarled, "Show me, Fargo. C'mon, now there's a referee, eh?"

Shocked faces around the circle were watching this tableau, and Fargo heard Julia cry, "Stop them! Somebody stop them!"

"He's been askin for trouble ever since he came aboard," Brimstone declared, "and this time, my good friends, he shall receive his just due."

Pickadilly Ike made a cackling sound. "Have at 'er, Skye, if you a mind to. Get drubbed, though, and it's your hard bacon."

Fargo was not particularly of a mind to, but realized his only other choice was to grovel his way out of camp like Brimstone demanded. That, of course, made him question what in hell was any sensible reason for staying. By then it was all a moot point anyway, for Logan roared, apparently enraged by Fargo's not responding. He drew himself back in a manner designed to make Fargo shrink before his tremendous size, and started forward, evidently expecting Fargo to retreat.

Instead, Fargo shifted his feet, took a half-step forward, and struck Logan with a right-left combo to the chest. Logan took the jolting blows, grunting twice, merely seeming to absorb the force of them. He swung a roundhouse haymaker that would have crushed Fargo's jaw, if Fargo hadn't been ready and danced aside.

Missing threw Logan off balance. He turned partly away, his belly unprotected, and Fargo hit him again. It was perfectly timed, a flurry of jabs to solar plexus and gut, and another right to the heart. But Logan remained on his feet. He absorbed punishment, and Fargo began wondering if anything short of a sledgehammer would put the man down and out. Logan, completing his turn, lost his footing and abruptly sat down. Before Fargo could attack, he twisted over on hands and knees, crouching like a sprinter.

"Never leave it said that I ain't proud to oblige when a man is a-wishing." He charged with his arms wide open.

Instead of meeting Logan directly, Fargo side-stepped at the last instant, figuring Logan would go past him. Logan was quicker than any man would expect. He turned and forced Fargo back. Retreating, Fargo delivered swift, short-range knucklers. There was no trick to hitting the big man, but it seemed futile, for Logan ignored the blow and kept advancing.

A wagon wheel gouged Fargo's back, the rim catching his heel. He tried to set his balance. Logan stormed in atop him. They caromed, fell, and rolled in the muck. Logan let his momentum carry him on and lurched upright, dragging Fargo along by the hair. Fargo butted him hard, breaking free. Logan swung his fist in a narrow arc, bending his arm at the final instant. The fist deliberately missed its mark and his elbow struck with the stunning power of a bludgeon.

Fargo felt the breath go out of him and staggered, smashing into the wheel again. He fell, landing on his back. A wild yell erupted from Logan, savage confidence lighting his face. Instinctively Fargo doubled both legs with knees beneath his chin as Logan came charging in. At the last instant, Logan comprehended and tried to stop, but he was too late. Fargo's legs uncoiled and snapped, his boot heels stabbing Logan in the pit of his stomach. Logan reeled, gasping and groaning, and crashed to the wet ground.

Brimstone and Rutherford had encouraged the settlers to cheer enthusiastically when Fargo hit the mud, but now that their man was down, their shouts grew lusty with calls to get up. Logan rolled sideways, scrambling to regain his feet in that waiting stance of his. Fargo straightened quickly, knowing Logan wouldn't stay crouched for long and thinking the fight must be fought differently. Body blows didn't hurt Logan, but those were the only shots open to a shorter man badly outweighed with a shorter reach. Scrutinizing Logan, Fargo was suddenly aware of his pristine nose and the lack of scars or any real damage to his features. Nobody ever had gotten to his face; Logan was just naturally ugly.

Fargo set himself, eyes sweeping the hungry crowd and glimpsing Rutherford leaning indolently against the wagon. Again Logan surged and again Fargo sprang aside. But this time Fargo jumped as well, angling a straight-arm punch higher, his fist crunching into Logan's cheek. The recoil jarred Fargo and sent pain stabbing through his arm, but when Logan pivoted, Fargo forgot the pain, seeing the flesh on Logan's cheek laid open in a long crimson furrow. Blood was dribbling down his face and he stood, tasting it, disbelieving.

Another charge and a drilling sock to Logan's left eye that gashed a cut in the brow. Logan, howling, reacted with instinctual swiftness, and before Fargo could evade the groping arms, Logan had him clamped in a bear hug.

Fargo felt his breath squeezed from his chest, pain sharp in his rib cage. Only his right arm was free of Logan's tightening vise, and it had no arc of motion and little strength. But a fury of desperation put force into the short pummeling jabs he landed behind Logan's ear. For a fraction of a second Logan's grip relaxed. Frantically Fargo wrenched away, sliding down through the band of arms, and skipped nimbly away.

Half-blinded by blood, Logan lumbered, pawing.

This was no time to chance being trapped by those arms again. Fargo leapt. The thrust of his own lunge, combined with Logan's rush, coalesced into a blow that hit Logan's chin with a jolting shock. Logan stumbled backward, and it was then, that instant, Fargo realized he had a glass jaw. A giant, a bull of strength, but with a jaw that betrayed. Immediately Fargo dived, pressing his advantage.

Logan had his hands partway up, looking at Fargo with blurred, half-comprehending eyes. If he saw the strike coming, he made no counter to fend it off. Fargo's left fist to the chin rocked Logan back on his heels. Fargo's blow launched Logan spinning and then collapsing flat on his face. He lay unmoving for a few seconds before slowly struggling to his knees.

Fargo headed for him. He knew the rules or the lack of them, knew that having his man down, he should kick and stomp him to a pulp. A moment ago, the settlers had been yelling for Logan to maul him. Now it was Logan who was vulnerable, and the whole sweating batch of them tensed for Fargo to claim his right. Logan watched Fargo, scrunching guardedly against an attack.

Instead, Fargo grinned scornfully and turned to walk off. It was, in its way, a worse insult than if he'd put his boots to the man.

"*Skye!*" Julia screamed suddenly. "Look out behind you!"

Pivoting, Fargo glimpsed Logan drawing his revolver. He sprang . . .

The revolver reared and exploded almost in Fargo's face. Eyes blurry, he made out the dark outline of Logan, and that was all he needed. He kicked out, catching the man in the face with the heel of his boot, sending him sprawling groggily in the mud. Then he scooped up Brimstone's whip.

"Now, back-shooter"—Fargo sounded so calm, Wyndam afterward swore he could not believe he was angry at all—"I'm going to give you a little something your parents should've given you a whole hell of a lot of years ago. I'm going to give you an old-fashioned horse-whipping that'll keep your pants afire for a week."

They must have heard the yell of terror and pain for a mile up the trail when the first stroke of four feet of the end of that long whip struck, Fargo holding Logan flat on the ground with his booted left foot jammed solidly down on the back of his neck. Logan fainted when the eleventh stroke fell, splitting the tight seat of his trousers from the crotch to the waistband as though a cavalry saber had landed a slashing cut back there. If he had expected sympathy or help in any manner from the settlers, he had not received it. The man had been beaten fair and square, and gunning while Fargo's back was turned went beyond the pale. They stood there popeyed, waiting for Fargo's fury to spend itself.

At last Fargo chucked the whip away and stood for a moment without moving. He stared at the limp thing on the ground, knowing everybody was watching him and not wanting to have to take Logan in hand again when the man returned to his senses. "And now," he finally said, "I'm going to go get cleaned off. The rest of you can root-hog here."

He ducked out of the circle, striding away quickly into the dark.

5

Skye Fargo knew something was wrong, something on top of everything else wrong with this loco outfit, but he couldn't quite get a handle on any of it. He was having a tough enough time getting a grip on his temper.

Ignoring the rain, he stalked from the camp toward one of the numerous creeks that fed the Boise River. A rush of water soon reached him through an intervening screen of brush and trees, and plowing through some entangling foliage, he found himself out on the creekbank, not far from where white-laced water cascaded through a clump of boulders, forming a small natural dam behind which swirled a clear, shallow pool. A few little animals fled when he approached through the grass, but otherwise the rock-screened area looked deserted.

Satisfied, Fargo stripped to the buff for a quick dip, eager to soak his bruises and cleanse himself and his clothes of the brawl's grime and blood. After stashing his gun belt and other personals under a stone overhang, he plunged from the crisp air into the cold water and began to harshly sluice clean. Squatting to his neck, he washed his face and hair and was dunking to rinse off when he heard the sound—and there was no mistaking it.

Julia Driscoll appeared at the boulders, pausing to

stand in their shadows, with her arms clasping a pile of clothes. "I didn't know if you had a clean change and I wasn't about to rifle your saddle bag looking. So I'm lending you some of Harold's duds," she said, smiling. "I also brought towels."

Instinctively Fargo crouched. "Thanks. Just put them with my belongings there in that rock niche."

Julia sighed, seeming reluctant to go. "The pond looks nippy but sure inviting, after tussling oxen all day." A lock of hair fell across one eye, which she flipped back with a toss of her head, a gesture Fargo found irresistibly attractive. Yet Julia was more than pretty; she was vital, independent, driving her own wagon, working like a man. "My, it's hardly the attitude for a widow, to think of herself now, not grieve over memories. I don't feel widowed. I feel changed, somehow, but not like a widow."

"We all change. Unavoidable. Besides, still water turns stagnant."

"Stagnant. Yes, that's the right word for it, for the way I was." She made a soft, odd sound in her throat. "The past two years, Harold grew sickly and neglected business, chores, everything, including me."

"You mean he didn't, er, you haven't . . . in two years?"

"Yes. That's why we were moving west, for his health."

"And yours. I'm sorry, Julia."

"So am I." She put her bundle in the niche and padded closer to the water's edge. She was totally nude. "But Harold was my choice, and we shared good times together that I'll cherish long after the rest has faded."

"Faded! To my eyes, the rest is standing here in bold, stark relief," Fargo allowed, involuntarily rising to the occasion.

"Not in relief, Skye, *for* relief." Her naked body was smooth and unblemished, her blackberry-nippled breasts swaying gracefully as she eased into the water. She waded closer, her pubic curls like a delicate froth accentuating rather than obscuring the fleshy crevice between her thighs. "Your face is bruised, poor dear, and your eyebrow is cut," she cooed sympathetically, and slid the palm of her hand along the rugged plane of his cheeks. "Let me make it better."

She kissed him, her hand sidling down between them toward his hardening erection. Even while calling himself a sucker, Fargo found himself kissing Julia back. She made a whimpering sound in her throat, still not breaking the kiss as she traced the thickening column of his aroused manhood.

"Cut it out," he protested huskily. "Everybody must know you've left. They'll worry, come looking. If we get caught by Brimstone or—"

"Then don't make me raise a loud stink, like I do when I don't get my way," Julia teased, silencing Fargo with a finger to his mouth. "It's either here or in my wagon, and we dasn't dare that. Oh, kiss my breasts, kiss 'em!"

This is crazy, Fargo thought. Yet hers was a blatant challenge, a passion de luxe, and what man could resist that? He kissed her lips, her cheeks, the tender hollow of her neck; then he bent lower to lave and suckle her hardened nipples. She moaned, her flesh melting to his liquid caresses, and her voice sighed in his ear, begging him to possess her completely and quench the long smouldering fires that now were rekindled in her belly.

"Be fast, be fast," she pleaded, straddling him there in the water. "Ahh, but how I'd adore having it last longer than it can."

Fargo pressed slowly, gently, and felt her stretching to accept him. He slid deeply up inside her, against increasing internal resistance. Her slim body trembled. She breathed raggedly through her mouth. "More, more . . . all of you . . . don't stop, yes . . ."

Glancing down at their merging loins in the dim pond, Fargo was gratified that she was managing to absorb him to the hilt. She had not been penetrated in years, yet she was enveloping his entire length and girth. Her eyes fluttered as his pelvis nudged against her mound, and she mewed soulfully as he withdrew slightly, his shaft moist with her secretions. Then he pumped back up into her, again and again, his tempo quickening while he embraced her supportively, and his mouth once again closed around her throbbing breasts.

Julia shuddered and gasped, whining, her words unintelligible but their meaning clear. She was urging him on, moving her hips in concert and helping to piston with increasing rapidity, breathless for her oncoming release. He drove furiously into her while she lowered her head, kissing his neck and nibbling his ears.

All of a sudden Fargo levered upward, freezing into quivering rigidity and erupting into orgasm, spewing hot and boiling into her depths as she twisted spasmodically with her own bursting climax. He deflated quickly, but she didn't move from astride him right away, continuing to hold him gently inside her.

She kissed him again. "Nice?"

"Damn nice," he murmured against her hair.

"Let's be nice again later." She smiled kittenish as she eased off him, and they started for the grassy edge of the pool. "My, it certainly is later," she remarked, a twinge of self-consciousness stealing over her as she walked for the boulders. "We better hurry, Skye. Pardon me while I go dress."

Fargo dug out the towel she had brought, and

despite the continuing shower, hastily dried as best he could and put on Harold Driscoll's clean clothes. They fit reasonably well; that and their well-worn age prompted him to think they dated from when Harold Driscoll had been well up to husbanding. There was a soreness all over Fargo's body, but strangely, he felt more invigorated after his erotic workout than before.

Julia returned wearing her workclothes and yellow slicker, looking fresh and proper as if the whole affair had been a figment of Fargo's sordid imagination. She eyed his bruised face again and clucked her tongue. "You had a whopper of a fight. Maybe I'm an alarmist, Skye, but I fear that high, low or foul, Gus Logan will try to pay you back."

"Yeah, he acted like one who'd nurse a grudge."

"Watch yourself." She stretched to give Fargo a peck on the cheek, then turned and headed trailward through the foliage. Fargo fell to following her, preferring to watch her blaze the way.

They entered camp separately from different sides. No one seemed to notice, the rain having driven the settlers into their wagons.

Fargo declined Pickadilly Ike's offer to share room inside his wagon, knowing it would be too cramped and that canvas, once waterlogged, could make the enclosed space suffocatingly humid. Instead, Fargo cadged a bottle of Dr. Seigismund's Magnetic Oil Tonic to ward off the chilblains, and bedded down under the wagon, whick luckily was parked on a low, well-drained hummock.

The rain was slackening to a leaden drizzle when Fargo roused. He lay still, listening for whatever had wakened him, then quietly slid from his sugan and inched across the buffalo robe that lay between bed-roll and ground. Shadow was black under the wagon. Somewhere a horse stomped impatiently.

The sound came again, a small squeak caused by a shifting of weight in wet leather boots. Fargo's hand wrapped around the butt of his Colt, peering intently, perceiving a vague outline. It was a deeper black than the diffused darkness of night, but could have been mistaken for part of the wagon's front wheel and steering gear, if it hadn't twitched restlessly. Then . . .

Knife steel flashed wickedly. Fargo lunged toward the figure, swinging his revolver, but the empty bedroll had warned the knifer and he leapt back. Fargo's lunge missed. The figure faded rapidly away into the showery night.

A dagger was buried haft-deep in the blankets. Fargo withdrew it and squatted, staring around the circle of wagons. Nothing stirred. Half a hundred yards out, a lone guard smoked quietly beneath his tented slicker.

Gathering his bedroll, Fargo climbed into the wagon and told Pickadilly Ike to move over, it'd gotten too cold to sleep outside.

During the balance of the night, the drizzle subsided to a sprinkle like a cold, breezy mist. Otis Wyndam's long-drawn call brought the camp awake while dawn was barely a pearlescent streak across the gunmetal eastern sky. Teams were brought in, harnesses thrown on, cookfires kindled ablaze.

Fargo saw to the needs of his Ovaro, checked his gear, and retied his bedroll on his saddle cantle, then took the knife from his belt and examined it closely. It was a fairly common quillon dagger, with a straight double-edged blade tapering from hilt to point, although this particular one boasted a silver-mounted bone grip.

Nodding thoughtfully, Fargo strode toward the Blutcher wagon. The aroma of boiling coffee steeped the chill air, Miracle tending both pot and frying pan while her father stoked the fire. Gus Logan was already there mooching breakfast, his face showing the marks of Fargo's fists. And as Fargo approached, he caught a peripheral glimpse of Abigail rounding the wagon arm in arm with Cheney Rutherford. Her expression, at the sight of Fargo, was as though she was suffering from ten ingrown toenails. Rutherford scowled and freed his right arm, his gun arm.

Fargo paid slight heed, focusing on Brimstone. The train boss saw him coming and straightened, stiffening. Fargo's grim smile was a quick, sharp break across his dark face as he threw the guillon dagger on the ground close beside Brimstone. Flickering flamelight picked out the silver tracery on the bone grip.

"It cut through my blankets. A shame it missed, eh?"

Gus Logan spilled his coffee. "What's that, Fargo?"

"Your knife, isn't it, Brimstone?" Fargo asked tightly. "It goes with that matching silver scabbard you pack on your belt."

Brimstone picked up the dagger. He hefted it absently, staring at Fargo. "How dare you insinuate I'd stoop to such deviltry. I lost this yesterday while prying my wagon out piece by piece from that bog hole. I—"

"Don't lose it again." Fargo turned to go and bumped against Rutherford, who had cut-footed in behind him. Abigail was there too, dour-eyed. Logan poised, hand on revolver, watching Rutherford for his cue. Miracle was shrinking back, silent, anxious, gnawing her lower lip. Fargo brushed roughly past Rutherford and stalked away, ignoring Brimstone's indignant calls.

While the ashen dawn lifted into an overcast morning, the settlers drove the small remaining stretch to the Snake River. From Glenns Ferry, they had taken the Boise River Valley route, not as a shortcut, but to avoid the original trail as it followed the Snake westward across arid volcanic desolation. The river then angled sharply north, coursing rampant through white-water rapids and deep, sheer gorges impossible to cross. The Oregon Trail's ford was far above the junction of its two routes, way up by the Payette tributary, where for a length the treacherous Snake was calmer and not compressed between chasm walls.

Other than the usual brief halts to water and feed the stock, the wagon train rolled steadily along the stone bluffs and scrubby copses paralleling the gorge. Along about evening, the trail wended lower as the banks softened into round, swaybacked slopes. The river widened, seeming to flow somewhat slower and gentler, yet its churning, rain-swollen torrent still made any crossing hazardous. And unfortunately where the track rose on the far side, the bank was overgrown with wild hawthorn, white fir, and pine, preventing wagons from pulling off or passing a breakdown.

On Wyndam's advice, Brimstone ordered a rest break before plunging on across and finding a campsite. The wagons formed a circle, as always, but the corral was merely to pen in stock, not to ward off Indians. After five days now, the scruffy Indian band dogging them since Fort Boise was as good as forgotten, except by Pickadilly Ike.

While the oxen grazed, the settlers had time to make simple repairs or grab a cold meal. Rutherford and Logan, swearing their wagon leaked rain like a sieve, began brushing black gum tar on the canvas cover, but soon quit to go eat at the Blutcher wagon, highfalutin' with Brimstone as brazenly as though they'd never been squelched.

Skye Fargo had little time to watch the goings-on. He'd been off hunting for much of the afternoon and was returning with a mule deer slung over his horse when he entered the wagon ring and caught sight of Otis Wyndam. The promoter was standing on a stump, an excited gleam in his eyes, a pair of field glasses in one hand, waving his arms at the settlers gathered around him in a gesture to command attention.

"M' friends, our goal ain't far now," Fargo heard Wyndam proclaim. "Mrs. Purvis here used my glasses to view the far bank, and her eagle eyes caught a blazed sugar pine at the ford. Once I spotted it, I knew it was the marker. Yep, a trail sign telling me that when we cross the Snake, soon's we strike yonder shore, we'll be trodding in Oregon country. Oregon! Bright news like that on a drab day oughta make a smile taste extra good on your lips."

It brought a chorus of cheers. They had traversed the Great Plains and South Pass. The broken, barren high prairieland along the Sweetwater and Snake rivers lay behind them, and so did the lure of Emigrant Pass and Californian gold, for the urge to till rich Willamette loam was a more compelling dream. The apparent nearness of their homesteads raised smiles on the gaunt faces of women and the harried lips of men who hadn't smiled in weeks.

Yet Fargo couldn't help wondering why Wyndam had needed a marker to tell their location. A man who'd traveled the trail before should've known that the Snake forms Oregon's eastern border, he thought while dismounting. It was then Fargo glimpsed Miracle Blutcher coming along the curve of wagons, wearing a twin of her ripped dress and threatening to bust seams out of this one too.

Fargo nodded as she approached. She stopped

close by, eyes soberly watching him unrope the deer carcass from his horse. Finally, hesitantly, she asked, "Did . . . did someone really try to kill you?"

"Either that, or they thought I like being knifed in my sleep."

"But why?"

Hesitating, he glanced about, then replied, "Ask your dad."

"Don't you dare say such," she snapped, bridling. "Pa knows nothing."

"True, not that it seems to stop him. So don't ask, or do, but it's to your dad you're going, Miracle, 'cause he's over there asking for you."

Turning, Miracle followed Fargo's gaze across the corral to the Blutcher wagon. Brimstone stood erect and high-shouldered by his dour wife, sending savage glares as loud and clear as any shout. Miracle nodded, though her eyes darkened and her smooth forehead showed a tiny furrowing.

"I wish they'd stop looking at me in that tone of voice," she grumped, moving to go, and took in a deep, heartfelt breath.

Fargo tensed, braced for a shredding burst of cheap muslin fabric. Somehow it kept whole and Miracle kept covered, if not overly modest, her firm bottom twitching saucily as she quickened her pace across the corral.

Poison honey, okay. Packed right and tight in a little ginger jar, but hell, he could admire the container without screwing off the lid, couldn't he?

Fargo gave the deer to a needy family, who with their friends would dress, salt, and share the venison. Soon after rose the call to hitch up again.

Dusky shadows were filling the gorge by the time Otis Wyndam led the wagon line splashing across the ford. Harnesses creaked and popped, whips cracked over the reluctant oxen, goading them to plunge, struggling, up to their bellies in the icy flow. The settlers plied more lash, impatient to reach the opposite bank. But Fargo was in no such hurry, having been to Oregon a time or two before and wanting to get there this time without breaking his or his horse's neck. He crossed slowly, cautiously, the Ovaro fighting for purchase on the slippery, sharp rocks, legs resisting the buffeting current.

Finally, one by one, the first wagons lurched out of the water, their teams pawing for a hold up the Oregon side and on along the trail. No problems there, Fargo thought, as long as nobody breaks down on the hemmed-in bank. He glanced back over his shoulder, saw the last of the wagons take to the river, and was thinking maybe the train would make it without mishap when he heard Julia Driscoll cry out.

Twisting around in his saddle, he saw her battling to control her teams, the oxen faltering, sliding broadside from the force of the surging water. She wavered, the reins tugging her reeling as if to topple, and she cried out again—but not in fright or hysteria, Fargo noted, wheeling his pinto so quickly that they almost keeled over. No, Julia was tongue-lashing her oxen with the lurid cussing of a veteran teamster, including some choice invectives that proper ladies were not supposed to know about, much less utter in screaming fits. Her oxen seemed to thrive on it, though, recovering their balance if not their wits, so it appeared to Fargo as he slewed in toward her wagon.

"Hang on!" He made a grab for the sideboard and missed.

"Hang on yourself," she retorted testily. Gritting her teeth with determination, Julia managed to regain control of her teams. When she rolled from the river and up the bank, she had again become the respectable widow, clean in thought, word, and deed.

Her pose gave Fargo a laugh. To be ruled by propriety, though, wasn't funny. He'd known women who never cared what something was, only how it looked, how acceptable it was, and they'd all been ballbusters. Any guy seeing behind their pose was a threat, to be crushed. Husband or lover, if a guy lost his standing, they'd turn on him, toss him over for someone in favor. Fargo didn't know how true this was of Julia, and didn't intend to find out.

At the moment, he wanted to find that trail marker. Remaining at water's edge while Julia went on ahead, Fargo began prowling at a walk, studying the mushy banks above and below the rocky strip that accomodated the ford. He soon located the sugar pine, that white pulp blaze on its trunk like a beacon against the dark-barked woods flanking the river and trail.

Dismounting, reins looped over his arm, Fargo moved to the marked tree as though in itself it could give him the answers he wanted. Idly, he reached out his hand and rubbed it over the white blaze. Gum lay stickily against his fingers. Frowning thoughtfully, he rolled some of it into a little ball, kneaded it, the fresh goo helping to increase his impression that something bad was hatching. A trail mark blazed by earlier immigrants would have long since dried. . . .

The wagon train camped a mile from the ford. Cool late evening closed around them as darkness flowed across the land, and campfires became winking stars in the night. Singing noised long and loud from the wagon circle, the settlers feeling they had much to rejoice. Why, they'd even shaken off that hounding band of old Indians, who'd refused to get wet crossing the Snake.

"Wasn't swimmin' they minded," Pickadilly Ike retorted. "Was meetin' the Northern Paiutes o'er here. Paiutes are lizard-eatin' coyotes who'll fill a man with arrows if they get him alone, and'll lurk in cutbank washes to haze your stock. I hear tell they've a taste for ox meat."

"You've heard a lot, Pickadilly, and told a lot more!" Rutherford, face stern, wagged a finger. "Keep your fears to yourself. We don't want upsettin' concerns bandied about that only raise alarm in the caravan."

Or, Fargo thought, that could raise alert.

Or suspicion. Like the business of the blanket raised in Fargo when he later returned from a final scout of the area. He saw the wet bedding from Rutherford's leaky wagon spread around the campfire, and Rutherford pick up a dried, khaki-brown blanket. But as Rutherford straightened, he let the blanket fall on the fire. He whisked it off quick and a cloud of thick, heavy black smoke hit the softer dark of the night sky. Then, in folding the blanket, he dropped it again. Three times it fell and three black plumes fingered high, illuminated from the campfire below. Smoke signals.

Fargo couldn't sleep after that. He lay in his bedroll under Pickadilly Ike's wagon, unable to find any answers and aware it was futile to keep trying. But still like a needle probing his body was that thread of worry he couldn't forget.

Then around one that morning, a shadow glided by in a swift, sneaky crouch.

6

Fargo began stalking the dark figure, curious as to his purpose.

He drifted around the corral perimeter, then broke into a sprint when he saw the figure dip between two wagons, racing outside the circle. Carefully he pressed to the shadowy bulk of the Conestoga behind him, scanning the rumpled terrain. His quarry was moving, easy to spot, although discernible merely as a silhouette under a wide-brimmed hat.

But that hat was a sufficient tip for Fargo. On its low crown, silver tinsel stars were weak yet noticeable glints even in this dim early-morning hour. Otis Wyndam. Fargo pursued on silent feet until he was reasonably certain that Wyndam was heading for the nearby horse cavvy. Then diving back to the corral, he angled up by Pickadilly Ike's wagon, where he'd staked out his Ovaro, hastily saddled, and walked the horse quietly toward the cavvy.

He was almost within earshot when he heard faint hoofbeats. Taking a gamble, he spurred northwestward in their direction, and as he rounded a cedar break, he caught a glimpse of Wyndam fading into the distant gloom. Launching into a gallop, chasing the cadence that echoed through the trees, Fargo felt a powerful hunch about what was happening and where it may lead. A day or two ago, someone slashed that sugar pine, wanting Wyndam to find it. Wyndam, on the lookout, would've kept it all a secret if Mrs. Purvis hadn't chanced upon the pine. He concocted his spiel of reading a trail marker to kill off curiosity and whump up enthusiasm, and he did well for on-the-spot shit-slinging. The blaze was a private sign, and now Wyndam was riding in response to it.

Fargo cut Wyndam's trail, finding sign fairly easily and following swiftly through the timber, Douglas fir and ponderosa pine covering the slopes when he climbed to higher elevations. A brisk forewarning of winter was in the air; it put energy into his pinto and he didn't take much time in crossing a small series of hogback knolls and dropping into a narrow canyon.

The course twisted and writhed in sundry directions as if in primeval torment, until shortly it split into two canyons. The hoofprints of Wyndam's horse were as gloomy on the canyon floor as Wyndam had been to him, and almost featureless on the hard-packed, rocky surface. Yet from scant sign, Fargo judged that Wyndam had chosen the left fork, so he headed along that route.

He perused his surroundings continuously, his ears tuned to catch the weakest noise. He detected what he thought were vague distant cries drifting along the defile, nearly inaudible and lacking clarity or direction. They gave him mixed feelings, for he sensed they were Indian, likely Northern Paiute, and that was a concern; but wherever they were gathered, it was some distance from here, and that was a relief.

The left fork unraveled circuitously, and Fargo was about to turn a blind corner when he perceived a second sound, like that of a low conversation somewhere close by. He reined in and sat waiting, motionless, listening, scrutinizing the canyon trail and sides and the wooded ridges above. Sharp as his eyes were, he wouldn't have glimpsed any telltale sign if it hadn't been for a delicate twist of breeze that brought him the faint odor of smoke.

The breeze died, but the single whiff had been sufficient. Anchoring his horse's reins under a rock, Fargo began to pad cautiously forward. He clung to the dreariest shadows he could find as he picked his way around the bend, gauging each bootfall as though he were treading on eggs, his eyes constantly roving, always on the alert.

He saw that the canyon broadened into an urn-shaped clearing strewn with boulders, bitter brush, and green manzanita. There was just enough space to hold a meeting in without stepping on one another's toes, and that was precisely what the four men ahead of Fargo were doing, grouped around a boxy large boulder that was serving as their table. Close alongside was a campfire, the obvious source of the trickling smoke, its pine-crackling flames shedding light across the boulder. The long roll of a map anchored by fist-sized stones was spread atop the boulder.

Otis Wyndam was among the men studying the map, his appearance in sharp contrast to his companions. The other three were roughly the same build—which was large—and wore denim pants scuffed white at the knees, and sweat-stained plaid shirts and jackets. They packed Smith & Wesson .44 revolvers in the old fast-draw army style, in plain leather holsters, butt forward and waist high on plain belts. Propped handily against the boulders beside them were three long guns of different lengths, models, and calibers. What distinguished the men from one another were their ages. They were fifteen to twenty years apart, Fargo estimated, judging by the amount of white hair on their matted whiskers. Son, father, grandfather . . .

On the far side of the clearing were their horses, heads drooping more from boredom, Fargo thought, than from exhaustion. He kept an eye on them too as he advanced on silent feet, hoping they wouldn't rouse to the sight and smell of him, or if they did, they wouldn't bother noising it around. He listened to the tone of the men's conversation, until finally he had sneaked in near enough to understand the words.

"I can't lollygag around here all night, Arvin," Wyndam addressed the middle-aged man, "and these maps have got to match." He had a rule and pencil and was carefully marking squares on the map as he talked. "Jessie, when you and Zeb get back to Portland, you make sure he buys a town suit and takes a bath, and have a barber trim your beard too. Looks like bird's nest. We want to impress these folks."

"You're puttin' me to a heap of hassle," Arvin grumbled. "Pullin' messy stunts like. Why didn't you get their money up front and skeddadle, not drag 'em here. Truth be, you should've just stuck to sellin' our parcels and making your records neat'n tidy, and been done with it. Then it's a cinch to shove 'em on down valley without a leg to stand on, like we always done before."

"I would've this time," Wyndam snapped, "if there hadn't been so many of them swarming in at the last minute, flinging offers at me with the cash to back them up. Turn those fools down, are you crazy? I signed them up to whatever they liked as often as they liked to, but look, all we got to do is doctor the maps so's everyone looks to have his own parcel. Then same's ever, you go claim it's your land, and they'll get nowhere but out, fast. If we don't do the maps, well . . ."

Fargo, watching hawkishly, saw Wyndam slit his throat with a finger. Then he felt something sharp bite through his shirt and nick his back. He had heard no sound, not the slightest, but there was steel against his spine.

"Stand up, arms up," he heard a voice mutter, "or die."

Fargo slowly, gingerly rose upright.

The four about the boulder straightened as well, startled. A disconcerted second later, three hastily snatched rifles were coming up on target, and Wyndam was beaming as if delighted Fargo could visit. "Well, well," he was saying, "well, well. It's quite rude to eavesdrop, y'know, and not very healthy, either. Umpqua, bring Mr. Fargo in."

The man behind Fargo completed his efficient, thorough check for weapons. The knife prodded, and Fargo moved up the path toward the slab-sided boulder. Wyndam was still smiling, but as Fargo approached, he glimpsed something that looked more genuinely helpful: rocks—specifically, the rocks anchoring the corners of the land map. If he could get his hands on them . . .

"We rarely take chances," Wyndam said, smirking. "Umpqua takes good care of us, in turn for a limited amount of whiskey and tobacco. He'll dispose of you speedily and simply, I promise you. You'll feel no pain, and the Snake will take your body."

Fargo said nothing. His face was stony as he moved toward the table.

Wyndam was still smiling. "Before he does, however, I'd like to know just how much suspicion you aroused back at the wagons. What made you follow us?"

"And if I don't feel like answering?"

"Then your death will not be so pleasant."

Fargo shrugged and moved an idle step closer. "Wyndam, since the start I've figured you'd had some shenanigan up your sleeve, so when I saw you skulk through the camp tonight, I guessed that maybe it'd be a good idea to follow along after you. But you got those folks eating out your hand, and there's not a soul figuring you're anything but square, I'm afraid."

"Them's music to my ears," Wyndam said heartily . . .

As Fargo reached for the nearest pair of stones . . .

And the man named Arvin yelped, "Watch—"

Hell broke loose, Fargo flinching as a slug from his own Colt ricocheted off one of the stones he grabbed, spraying him with rock chips. As he twisted, he saw that Wyndam was closest, and he smashed the rock in his right hand full in the land shark's mouth. He saw Wyndam start down but not land, for lead from Arvin's .44 slit his shirt cuff, stinging a furrow across his wrist, prompting Fargo to turn and throw the rock that had felled Wyndam straight at Arvin.

Arvin attempted to duck, triggering in his haste and almost blowing a hole through his foot. Fargo had grown up playing at tenpins, learning to pitch accurately, and the stone beaned Arvin smack on the bridge between his eyes, which abruptly crossed as he flopped backward over another boulder.

Umpqua's knife began slashing the air as he leapt across the clearing with the speed of a mountain puma. Fargo twisted, scooping up and hurling another rock from the table. It caught Umpqua flush in the mouth, choking off what he started to say, the Indian plummeting to the ground in a spray of blood and shattered teeth.

Zeb was tracking Fargo with a 12-gauge Greener, finger-squeezing the trigger. Unfortunately for him, Fargo had glimpsed him peripherally and was already tossing another stone, adding enough knuckle to give it a little hook. The stone curved in and struck Zeb on the left temple. He fell over, landing hard and accidentally discharging the Greener into the sky. It created a great amount of noise and smoke, causing no harm, but distracting Jessie.

And Jessie was the only one left between Fargo and the freedom of the night. His fist was hard as the rocks he'd flung, and Jessie had his chin out and his guard down. Fargo felt the shock of his punch run clear to his shoulder, and he watched Jessie arch backward and slide five feet along the ground, coming to rest when his head struck the flat boulder.

They were all down, temporarily.

Fargo sprang from Umpqua, rifling the Indian and recovering his knife and revolver. Umpqua was making movements now, and Fargo could hear grunts and groans from some of the others as he bounded for the canyon. He reached the edge of the clearing when a shot from behind him traced a path between his feet. He veered toward the bend ahead, dashed around it, hearing a lot of calling back and forth and an occasional gunshot. He also heard his Ovaro stamping nervously, and the sound guided him to his mount.

He stepped into leather and sent his pinto streaking down-canyon for the cover of dense timber. A long gun roared faintly behind him, but the range was off. He did not bother to look back. He knew they would come. Anywhere, any angle, not just from behind, for they knew the country and knew he'd head for the wagon train. They would have to come and would persist with a dogged, brutal tenacity until either he or they were dead, but one advantage lay with him: they would have to come to him.

The Ovaro raced into the trees and Fargo kept it

going until it had sped up a slope. The timber was thicker here, but he deliberately crossed a patch of open ground where the horse hooves made visible imprints, and when he was beyond it, he made a circle and doubled back. He came to a small depression and, dismounting, settled himself and the horse down away from casual view. Somewhere in the timber an owl called, a mournful quaver. After a while it was very still and a solemn silence settled over the woods.

Fargo waited with his Sharps. Once he thought he heard a twig snap and this brought him sharply alert, but he caught no repetition of the sound. When at last it came again, there was no doubt as to its reality. Fargo propped the Sharps against his shoulder and squinted down the long barrel at the open patch.

After Fargo waited for what seemed an interminable stretch of time, Zeb came into view. He moved slowly and cautiously, alternately studying Fargo's tracks and the trees. He started across the patch, carrying his rifle out in front of him in such a position that he could whip it instantly to his shoulder and snap off a shot, and when he was in the center of the patch, Fargo fired.

The report of the Sharps was loud and throaty in the silence of the timber. The echoes went rolling through the canyon with a lingering reluctance. Zeb jerked spasmodically and dropped abruptly on both knees. His chin fell and it looked like he was going to pitch forward on his face when he suddenly caught himself. His shoulders squared, his head started to lift, and the rifle began coming up in his hands. Fargo was hurriedly reloading the Sharps when Zeb suddenly slumped and toppled over. He lay with his face shoved in the earth, which soaked down his blood as fast as he spilled it.

Suddenly a gun began to bark down in the trees, throwing a stream of bullets at Fargo. Slugs wailed shrilly as they ricocheted off stone, and he was forced to draw back, the bullets continuing until the man in the trees had emptied his rifle.

When the shooting ceased, Fargo edged forward and chanced a quick look, but he couldn't see anything in the timber. It had sounded like one gun down there and Fargo drew back again and mulled it over. They were splitting up down there, he bet, trying to catch him in a cross fire. He thought a little more on it and then he left the depression, leading his Ovaro.

There was more timber ahead, although the trees were not so dense here, and Fargo headed for this. Several slugs shrieked through the brush, clipping twigs and leaves in a whining fury. He sprang onto his saddle and darted forward, ducking low to avoid branches, and the firing soon tapered off, leaving him moving cautiously along in tree-canopied gloom. He scanned the forest until his eyes ached, and always there was nothing to see.

Then, gently reining, he dismounted, gripping the Sharps tightly. Someone was moving along the windfall on the other side. He could hear the soft scrape of cloth against the timber and against the ground, then the sound of muted breath, and he ever so lightly eared back the gunhammer.

Suddenly, not five feet from Fargo, a head came over the top of the windfall. The shoulders appeared also and then Jessie was staring directly at Fargo. Horror and imminence of the inevitable distended Jessie's eyes and contorted his features. His mouth gaped wide as he prepared to shout, but Fargo blew his brains out before he could utter a cry. He pitched forward, jerked convulsively once, and then was still.

The muscles were quivering with reaction in Fargo's belly as he built another load for the Sharps. This left three more, he was thinking, but this ridge was not good anymore. Action makes attraction.

Once again he remounted and started through the trees. Presently the gray of an open area showed ahead, but he stayed in the fringe of the timber as he circled the clearing, eyes studying the rim of trees across from him. He came to a brook after that and dropped on his belly and drank avidly. Beyond the brook, the land dropped abruptly and Fargo halted in the cover of two cedars growing close together and pondered the country beyond.

After a short hesitation, he lifted his horse into a hard run. The Ovaro's hooves made a sharp, drumming crescendo as it galloped across the hardpan and rocky soil that lay southeastward to the wagon train.

7

There was a suspicion of gray, the false dawn, in the sky by the time Fargo caught sight of the wagon train. To his relief, he had not run into further trouble on his return, and as a guess, he figured maybe the others had cut their losses at two dead, and cut for safety while they still had time.

In any case, Fargo saw the sparkle of yonder firelight across the dark terrain and pressed his flagging horse toward the encampment. The sound of predawn rising, the smell of boiling coffee and flapjacks filtered through to him as he approached. Then, spurring between wagons into the corral, Fargo glimpsed the familiar features of Otis Wyndam over with a group of settlers.

Eyes turned toward Fargo, and voices were rising as though by one accord: "There he is! Get him! Before he can do any more harm!"

Fargo reined in sharply, dismounting woodenly, and he hardly saw the arms reaching for him. "What this all about—" he began, and then settler men, with hands hard from labor, were grabbing at him.

Brimstone Blutcher thrust his beadle's face toward Fargo. "I'll tell you what this's all about," he thundered sonorously. "You deserted us. Sold us out, you did, traffickin' with Satan. You went off and conspired with men who own many acres o' Oregon land. You plotted to hornswoggle us into buying it instead of the honest acres Mr. Wyndam has to offer. Then your scheme was to skip with our money when those men came to reclaim their land. But, fortunately for us, Mr. Wyndam saw you ride off t'night, and he followed and overheard your confab. He returned as fast as he could, to warn us of your duplicity. Consider yourself our prisoner."

Fargo listened to Brimstone's scathing denunciation, and the words were like something out of a nightmare. While he'd been fighting for his life, Wyndam had beaten him to camp and now was accusing him of the treachery he had planned himself. "You can't—"

"That's what you think," one of the settlers holding him growled.

Fargo twisted, trying to break free, draped in men. He tore them off and they tore back on, and for each one he flung aside, another leeched a hold, trying to drag him down while he stumbled and staggered in his bid to escape. Their yelling, cursing, scuffling pandemonium spurred other men who'd been standing about, and they joined in to add their weight.

Parrying a punch with an uppercut, Fargo slammed a knee into another attacker's groin while chopping the side of his hand across someone else's face. Two men tackling him were snagged, one by each of his fists, and then their heads were bashed together. Before they had fallen, he was mauling yet another man, fighting to break out, an experienced brawler who was pissed off and refused to be taken easily.

But the settlers finally engulfed Fargo. Sweaty, dusty, angrily misguided, they surged in while Fargo battled back using hands, elbows, knees, his entire body as a weapon. He got clobbered in a vise of three men, six sets of knuckles landing simultaneously. As Fargo reeled back, dazed, Otis Wyndam came in from behind and pistol-whipped him with the butt of his revolver, the vicious blow to the head dropping Fargo to the ground.

Dimly, as if through a swirling fog, Fargo heard Wyndam's voice: "Too bad, but necessary. Our little group must be rid of troublemakers like Fargo, even at the tall cost of death. We must all pull together."

Those were fine words, and they were bitter as gall and as false, Fargo thought groggily, but there was no rejoinder he could make, the hammering crack on his skull having paralyzed him from head to heel. Unconsciousness was coming, yet oddly it was not here yet. He could still see, dimly, and hear.

Cheney Rutherford bent over him. "He's still breathing. Get— "

"We cannot have such a man loose in our camp!" Wyndam, reversing his revolver, thumbed its hammer. "I brought him in, and I'll take him out—"

"No!" Rutherford countered sharply above the gasping cries of a few women and the hoarse voices of men, one of whom called, "Leave him be, Otis. We owe Fargo all the trouble we can make him, but we got troubles enough, without killing."

"Later on we'll try Fargo, and if he's guilty, we'll hang him," Rutherford suggested. "Fair and square. Nobody can squawk about it that way. Except maybe Fargo."

Another wave of unconsciousness was sweeping over Fargo, and he tried to fight it with all the power of his will as he was tied hand and foot. He was laid on a buffalo robe beneath the nearest wagon, his legs tied to each hind wheel so he could not wriggle away. Two men were stationed with rifles to watch him.

Gradually he recovered his senses. His body, especially his rib cage, throbbed with pain, and his head pulsed with an excruciating ache. He fought his bonds until his arms and legs all but broke from the strain, but there was no give to the ropes.

Resting, hoping to regain some strength, he eyed the two guards as they swapped dirty jokes. One of them sauntered toward a cookfire to get a cup of coffee. The other stood up, yawning audibly. Gus Logan came and spoke to the one remaining guard, and as Fargo watched, he felt a slackening in the ropes that held his legs. He half-turned, expecting to feel the knife bury in his chest. A hand touched his lips warning him to silence, a soft, soap-scented hand. Knife steel sawed the bonds about his arms. Then he was free.

"A horse is staked just out a ways," Miracle Blutcher whispered. "They're watching yours too close in case you try to escape. You'll have to use this one. Take it, Skye, take it and ride—"

Cheney Rutherford coughed, and at the sound Miracle faded silently back into the night. Cautiously Fargo worked his limbs until the free flow of circulation returned. Moving his arm, he found that Miracle had left him the knife. He crawled away from the wagon, creeping out toward the dim void of open land beyond the circle, then rose to a crouch and sprinted to where a saddled chestnut mare was placidly grazing.

So far no one had tried to stop him, and he scowled in puzzlement. The mare was hock-scarred but appeared in fair condition, certainly good enough for his quick flight. Pulling its picket pin, he began leading the horse away. Had he been mistaken about Miracle, or Rutherford? Or was Rutherford . . .

Abigail Blutcher's unmistakable voice screamed

shrilly. "Brigham! Oh, oh, he's dead! Brigham's been stabbed."

Fargo started to fling himself across the horse and ride for it, then he stopped. Back at the wagons he could hear Rutherford's wild yell! "Fargo, he bust free!" It was followed by a rising tumult of shouting. He weighed his chances in that few seconds and made his irrevocable choice. He slapped the chestnut mare with the picket rope and sent it clattering away across the murky field.

"There he goes! He's gettin' away!"

Settlers ran after the horse, firing blindly.

Fargo raced back toward the wagons, there to skulk in the shadows, listening, watching.

"Was that dratted Skye Fargo, it must've been," Abigail was sobbing.

Otis Wyndam shook his head. "A shame, a pitiful shame, Miz Blutcher. I never dreamed the emnity between him and your husband would come to this."

A clever touch, Fargo thought angrily. The settlers would be quick to remember the bitter words and that fight between Brimstone and himself, and be quicker to condemn him as a vindictive, cold-blooded murderer.

Dawn was lightening the horizon now, stretching shadows, although visibility was still limited. Horses were caught up as half a dozen men set out in grim pursuit. The remainder stood cussing.

"Kill him on sight," Rutherford declared sternly. "Maybe we should've listened to Wyndam instead of to me, and shot him like a mad dog."

Fargo had chanced to come in by Rutherford's wagon. He dared go no farther. Loosening one edge of the half-tarred canvas cover, he slid beneath it, wriggling down between the thick cases of the load.

Men's voices came to him. Boots pounded. He felt someone climb across the front of the wagon.

"Finish tarring that tarp at the breaks today, Gus," Rutherford's voice said. "We're getting close to the breed. He'll be watching for this wagon with the black top."

Fargo stiffened. He listened carefully but could hear nothing more. After a time the wagon jolted as the teams were hitched. Then came Otis Wyndam's drawn-out call and they began to roll out. The black tar coating absorbed sunlight, and heat built up inside the wagon. A fine dust sifted up through the bed floorboards. Thirst cloyed at Fargo's throat, but there was not a damn thing he could do about it or his battered, aching body.

At ten the first stop was made. Somebody began daubing at the canvas with a tarry brush. Wyndam's voice came to Fargo.

"He get away?" Rutherford asked.

"They found the horse some three miles out," Wyndam said. "Nary a trace of Fargo. Might not get as far as he hopes, but plumb quick lose his head, at least his scalp. Pickled-liver Ike claims there's Paiute sign thicker than bluegrass around here, but then, he would."

"For once I hope the old soak's right," Rutherford commented. The voices grew fainter as the men walked away.

Shortly the train moved on. They did not stop for a long "nooner" or siesta, as would've been done during hot summer or in the Southwest, but drove until two in the afternoon. Fargo lay very still and quietly went crazy as the odor of cooking food wafted inside. After a time a hand rattled the loose edge of the cover where he'd crawled into the wagon.

"Tighten this tarp, you fool," Rutherford's voice rasped. "Want someone poking around our load?"

The cover was drawn taut and fastened. Again they started out, and as the wagon jounced rattling through an eternity of heat and dust, Fargo grew increasingly curious about the load. He began poking. Except for bedding and other obviously personal belongings, the load consisted of large rectangular wood crates that, when he shifted some, proved so lightweight as to be empty. He settled back to ponder transporting a load of empty crates, and dozed off.

When Fargo came awake, the joggling had finally ceased. He lay famished and listless while Rutherford pitched in to help Logan complete the tarring.

"That's enough, Gus," Rutherford said at last. "C'mon, let's go make our appearance at the gawdawful singsongy. You'd think with Brimstone croaked, they'd kill it off too."

"Wal, p'raps Miracle will hit a high note and dump her dress."

"Better not, else we'd all go blind." Rutherford chuckled lewdly. "But remember, when the time comes, we can't play no favorites, leave no witnesses."

Skye Fargo fingered his knife in helpless fury, listening to the two men walk away. Soon the songfest began with "I Dwelt in Marble Halls," but Fargo waited till they'd warmed up with a few more ditties and were belting out "Onward Christian Soldiers" to the accompaniment of Pickadilly Ike's banjo. He then slashed one corner of the tarp and thrust out his arm, finding a tie rope and slashing it as well. Out he wriggled. He roped the cover down and hastened away.

After the singing ended for the night, Pickadilly Ike lumbered back to his wagon and, grunting wheezily, hoisted himself inside. He set his banjo aside and was reaching for a bottle of tonic when he paused, then sat back on his haunches. "Mister," he told his buffalo robe, "you're in powerful trouble."

"I know," the robe said, belching, and flopped about in the cramped space as Fargo crept out from underneath. "I think your beef jerky was rancid."

"There're worse ways to die." Pickadilly Ike uncorked a tonic. "This's one, an' you're skirtin' the rest," he said after a swallow. "Now, what goes on in here ain't nobody's business 'cept ours. If your brains ain't addled, let us get to the straight of things."

Fargo recounted following Wyndam, concluding, "He switched the facts and tried to kill me so the truth wouldn't be believed or discovered. I've a hunch that although Zeb and Jessie are dead, greed is thicker than blood, and Arvin still will show up claiming to own your land after Wyndam's got your money. No telling how many times they've pulled the same shenanigan on settlers."

"This'll be their last whirl," Pickadilly Ike growled. "All we've got to do is grab Arvin, or whoever, and make him admit the flimflam. Now, what say concernin' Brimstone? The gent was insufferable, but Skye, you didn't—"

"Damn sure, I didn't! Someone else stabbed him and trapped me double." Explaining that led Fargo to relate the talk he'd overheard while in Rutherford's wagon, the empty crates and the smoke signals. "I don't know where or when, other than soon, or who, except for the breed. But it stinks of a raid, a setup for a massacre."

"Ain't heard o' Northern Paiutes doin' it afore, but Lawd knows Injuns cahooting with whites have wiped out many a wagon train. Also puts sense to Rutherford poo-pooin' my cautions with lullaby talk."

Pickadilly Ike swigged again and began to grow rosy-cheeked. "Well, if what you claim is true—"

"*If what I claim is true!*" Fargo balanced himself, ready to lunge at the first hostile move. "If you don't believe me . . . If I made a mistake, and you're in with Wyndam or Rutherford, you and me are going to have it out."

Pickadilly Ike leaned forward a little, assuming a half-crouch, as he whisked out a wicked-looking Arkansas toothpick knife from his boot top. "Don't figger to carve you up, friend, 'less I have to."

Fargo checked the rash impulse to make a fight of it. Pickadilly Ike went on drawling, testing the keenness of the knife blade with the ball of his thumb. "Scout, buffalo hunter, Injun fighter, but never been a spellbindin' orator, and you ain't neither. Ain't no use tryin' to convince folks what you claim is true. They've listened to Wyndam too long, and Rutherford, so they'll have to be shown when, if you can get proof. Before they get you."

Fargo laughed mirthlessly and reached for the bottle. "That's a chance I'll have to take."

That night and all the next day, Fargo hid in Pickadilly Ike's wagon. Gradually the light faded and the train halted for another night. He was somewhat familiar with this campsite, for it was conveniently near Farewell Bend, the last spot where the Oregon Trail passed within eyeshot of the Snake River. The site itself was a large bowl-shaped field, rimmed by trees, with a great heap of boulders in the very center.

"Corral around the rock, gents! Makes a fine safe place for our stock," Wyndam called down the line, "and it's better to have it close by to watch, and not out always, letting some damn-fool redskin creep up behind."

They ringed the rock. Fargo heard the bustle of settlers making camp, the older kids hunting the woods for kindling and cones, and young ones playing on the tumbled stone mound.

Soon Pickadilly Ike snuck him some food, looking disgruntled. "I'm whiffin' somethin' rotten goin' on. Rutherford suggested this place to Wyndam, which's nice enough, 'cept the wagons ain't touching close together 'cause the rock is too big 'round. Nobody sees a need. Nobody sees any Injun, and Rutherford, him and Logan say there ain't been any clashes here in years." His gnarled hand scratched his scarred face. "I dunno. All this lovey-dovey peace is a bad sign to me. Fits my luck to draw horse guard t'night. Tell you true, Skye, I won't sleep too well on my shift."

Fargo smiled. "I hope you don't. It'll be a good change."

In time the land grew silent, a dusting of cool stars and a meager crescent moon hidden as much as not above a screen of fast-flowing clouds. Gradually the fires within the corralled wagons dwindled, the sound of talk died away. . . .

"Wake, Skye, wake up!"

It was close to two in the morning when that trembling hand and Pickadilly Ike's husky whispers aroused Fargo. Cloud streamers were skimming low and there was a hazy murk in the sky when, cramming his shirttail and wrenching on his boots, Fargo followed the old-timer outside. An old Starr .44 gleamed dully in Pickadilly Ike's hand as he thrust it butt-first toward Fargo.

"Here. Don't ask where I borrowed it."

Fargo didn't ask, merely grinned his thanks while sliding the Starr into his holster, filling the gap left by his confiscated Colt revolver. They hastened toward a stretch of the woods that was on a low, slender rise like an overgrown earthen fence wall. At its far side was the horse cavvy where Pickadilly Ike had been on guard; in between was a strip where Fargo could hear gravel rolling down an ancient rockslide.

Pickadilly Ike grabbed his arm in a grip that made him wince, "There, Skye," he muttered. "There!"

And then Fargo saw Miracle Blutcher scrambling toward him, eyes big and wild even in the dim light, and her face as colorless as a sheet. In a moment her outstretched hands were clutching his shirtfront, her head dipping to his shoulder, her mouth gasping, almost sobbing. He put arms about her, even while wondering why he'd comfort poison honey who'd already stung him once.

"You, h-here," she faltered. "Ike said you'd come, help me . . ."

"Miz Blutcher is back o' the rise," Pickadilly Ike explained gravely, his face looking a yard long. "Her throat's been slit, ear to ear. I ne'er heard a thing anywheres, not till Miracle let loose a yelp."

"Nothing to hear, probably. It's a quick, quiet way to kill." Fargo lifted one hand to tilt the girl's chin up so he could look into her terror-stricken face. "You've suffered hell lately, caused some, too. Now, what's gone on?"

"A little while ago something awoke me. My stepmother wasn't there." Miracle glanced toward the wagons. "I'm sure she'd been drugging our tea at night. I'd pour mine out if I got the chance, but Pa wouldn't believe me. I shouldn't have believed her about cutting you free, Skye. She tricked me, honest, her and Cheney Rutherford."

Plus Gus Logan, Fargo suspected, to actually do in Brimstone.

"I can't say I hated Cheney. He was trying hard to

take Abigail away from Pa, and by grab, I've been pining for some chump to do that." Miracle turned back, nuzzling Fargo's chest. "No doubt they thought they'd doped me asleep. I must've been dead out at first, 'cause when I looked around for Abigail, I discovered the floor hatch pried open, and the strongbox missing from the well under the wagon bed."

"Strongbox?" Fargo pressed. "The one holding everyone's cash?"

"That's right. Pa and Mr. Wyndam hid it there, just like they had done when Mr. Driscoll was train boss. So I figured now that Pa was dead, Abigail and Mr. Rutherford were stealing off with the box before another boss was elected and it got moved again. I headed for the horse cavvy and . . . and found her there alone, no box, all bl-bloody and . . ." Miracle choked, whimpering.

Pickadilly Ike fumed, "Rutherford, Logan, them lice are far gone—"

"You'd have heard their horses leaving," Fargo countered. "No, I think they'll stick around for their job with this breed. That's the reason they joined our outfit. Rutherford must've learned of the box from Abigail, who lusted for both, then saved me from Wyndam when he saw how to get it, Brimstone dead, and me blamed. He and Logan cut out Abigail, hid the loot, and I bet won't cut in the half-breed. This had to be timed for when the big job would cover their theft, before camp or crook caught wise. Now's time, dammit. Take Miracle back and roust everyone, Ike, and watch everything, every which way."

"Aye, y'mean like how those dumb nags are actin'?"

Fargo peered across the darkness to the cavvy. He knew the first moment some horses stopped grazing or nodding adoze; he knew soon as they perked their heads toward the wagons circling the huge rockpile. "Hell, yes," he snapped. "They're not dumb. C'mon, hurry!"

They rushed the short distance to the camp. Fargo charged straight ahead, hefting his borrowed revolver and calling himself a damn fool again, wondering if the rusty old .44 would explode in his face before or after the settlers began shooting him on sight. Miracle veered toward her wagon to grab a weapon, she said, though Fargo hoped she'd stay under cover. He'd feel safer.

Pickadilly Ike ran zigzagging as he scavenged a half-dozen long pine knots. Moving on, he was near behind Fargo when they headed between wagons. Then Fargo saw him pausing for just a moment, to scrape the beeswax off a Swedish match, fire it, and light one of the pine knots. There was no wind, and the wax helped hold the flame, but mostly it was the resin coating on the knot that, despite the recent rains, ignited like parched dry tinder.

Fargo, dashing into the corral, glimpsed shadowy figures afoot sneaking in on the wagons from around the rock mound. Pickadilly Ike was leaping after him, fanning the pine torch and kindling the other knots, one after another, launching them in high, flaming arcs over the camp. Just when the dark figures were ready to strike sleeping victims, right when a dozen or so were closing in to stab and chop, an alarm more effective than any signal was spread by the blast of an old percussion pistol, six fiery comets sailing through the sky, and a rheumy codger's shout as piercing as a raspy bugle call: "Men, if you love your children and your women, if you love your lives—here's light, so you can see where to shoot!"

Yes, there was light. Two wagons were suddenly burning. Women and children began screaming and men cursing and yelling orders as the wagon train came alive. A dozen or more figures in feathers and beads, painted all over in red and yellow and black stood like frozen nightmares, each with a dark lantern and each with a knife or hatchet.

Fargo sighed a satisfied "Ahh" to himself, and it acted like a cue to Pickadilly Ike as well. Two shots roared as one, and two figures went down like the sitting ducks they were. After that it grew more confusing. With startled howls and grunts, the rest of the men sprang to defend themselves, some digging smaller .36 and .38 pistols out of breechclouts and returning fire, all scrambling desperately for shelter.

Three settlers were wounded almost at once, and a rather stout matron was punctured through her rump. She sat down, hard, but as much from the recoil of her Kentucky turkey rifle as from her injury. Her rifle ball bowled over the middle man of three who were ducking for the rock heap. The second man was plugged in the kidneys by the Rasmussen boy, and the third raised his pistol and triggered at Fargo the same instant Fargo shot at him. A settler who chanced to be scuttling past Fargo gave a half-twisting lurch, as if grazed along the hip or over the ribs. Fargo's truer aim snatched the third man off his legs, the bullet smashing into his cheek.

The man landed on his knees, hands clawing at his face, head wobbling as if shaking to deny he was dead. His scraping fingers gouged furrows of paint off his skin, and pulsing blood was washing away more. Then someone recognized him as Gus Logan. Instantly the settlers comprehended what the knifes and dark lanterns were for. The circle of thunderous guns pursued the white-man Indians like an avenging tidal wave.

With yells of shock and pain, the vicious attackers dived up into the rocks, or tried to fight past and escape between the wagons. The determined settlers thrust them back, despite their frenzied attempts to burst out of this ring of death. Shots cracked, knives snicked, hands grappled for throats. Otis Wyndam whacked his rifle across an attacker's face and almost bent the barrel. The man fell away in a spew of teeth and blood, his countenance mashed in like a wash-tub. Fargo emptied the old Starr in short order, traded it in for a rifle a wounded settler had dropped, and emptied it too. Then he used it as a club as he searched for a replacement. He accidentally kicked Pickadilly Ike as he was wrestling with an attacker as raving made as he; when next the attacker was glimpsed, his head was missing, for Ike had scooped up a hatchet and was slashing at painted bellies and limbs.

Gradually resistance from the attackers lessened as their firearms emptied and their numbers dwindled. The survivors could withstand just so much punishment and frantically scurried higher, deeper into the jumbled boulders. They were fearful to behold, blackened with powder as well as paint, smeared with blood and dirt. Yet they were dislodged time after time, forced to retreat farther, hard-pressed to keep up with the settlers. If these men and women were stubborn and courageous under attack, they were absolute terrors in defense of their homes, their wagons.

The pitifully few attackers that remained were bottled up in the rocks, fighting on like the cornered rats they were. The battle finally wound down to close-quarter melees of knives and hand-to-hand skirmishes. One maddened man rushed at Fargo with a bowie. Pickadilly Ike cried, "I'll git 'im," angling in with his short-barrel blunderbuss. His hammer fell with a metallic click.

Fargo was already stepping back a pace to aim and fire, again armed with a discarded revolver, this time a J. H. Dance & Bros. .44 Dragoon, which some gunmen swore by and others swore at. Fargo plain swore as he triggered, the Dance .44, plugging the man so close that the muzzle flame scorched his painted chest.

Muttering disappointment, Pickadilly Ike came over fiddling with the flash pan of his blunderbuss. "Damn primer got wet again." By the time he had the pan freshly loaded and the flintlock cleared, the fighting had abated, and all he and Fargo could view were the dead attackers and live settlers through stinging, sulfurous black powder gunsmoke.

Pickadilly Ike stretched. "Well, that it?" he asked.

A rifle burst shattered the momentary lull. Pickadilly Ike sobbed as his body jerked around, and withered slumping at Fargo's feet. Fargo crouched, one glimpse telling him the old scout was dead, and he swiveled around searching with blood rage in his eye. There—a movement, furtive and quick, over by Rutherford's tarred-top wagon, a glimpse of dark painted skin and blond hair.

"Rutherford! Son of a bitch!"

Revolver in hand, Fargo vaulted around edges of boulders in a wild bounding descent down the mound. He surged across the level, hunkering low at one point as he ran, to see if he could spot Rutherford hiding beneath or behind his wagon. Nothing. Now Fargo feared he'd not been in time, that somehow Rutherford had managed to steal a horse and had already fled. Diving around the front of the wagon, staring ahead toward the open country beyond the ring, he was caught off guard by the sudden, unexpected emergence of Rutherford from inside the wagon.

Rutherford seemed equally startled. Having sprang atop the end gate, he teetered for an eyeblink, seemingly stunned by the sight of this snarling man, unnerved at the thought of Fargo returning from his death trap to deal retribution. Right hand fisting a revolver, his left holding a pair of saddlebags balanced on his shoulder, Rutherford jumped to the opposite front wheel. He pivoted, firing, with violent swiftness, then dropped to the ground. Fargo ducked behind the corner, then dipped right back out again, aiming the Dragoon. The different heft and grip felt strange yet damn good to him, and he moved to return a lead memento to Rutherford, cursing as his bullet splintered wood of a wheel spoke where Rutherford's head had just been. He went around the front again, vaulting the tongue, scanning for Rutherford.

Rutherford stood not twenty yards away, busily trying to shove the slipping saddlebags back on his left shoulder so he could unencumber his gun hand. The bags slid some more, and seeing Fargo, Rutherford let them drop to the ground. One bulging bag hit on its bottom corner, jamming the contents against the flap, the force unraveling the poorly tied strap. Money flopped out, wads of loose bank notes in every denomination, stacks more in paper bands of many colors.

"The strongbox cash, eh?" Fargo, lunging, laughed caustically. "It's killed you, you greedy bastard, it's bought you a grave."

His face full of fright and fury, Rutherford tracked a bead on Fargo. He turned fast, fired fast—too fast, too soon, his bullet straying wide.

Ignoring it, Fargo kept on coming. He thought of

Brimstone and Abigail, of an orphan girl, of untold victims butchered for their simple possessions, and of Indians who undoubtedly got blamed and killed because of it—and he triggered the unfamiliar Dancer Dragoon coolly, deliberately before Rutherford shot again.

Rutherford slapped both hands to his chest, blood pumping from between his fingers. He stumbled blindly in a half-circle, to lurch hard against the wagon. He wavered and sank down in a sitting position, his death-rattling gasps bringing blood to his lips. "Damn you," he choked, and said no more.

Fargo looked at Rutherford, then at his revolver, which was empty, then walked back to the front of the wagon. One down and two to go, he told himself. He had Wyndam to nail, a squirmy fast-talking gypster with all the settlers siding him. So he had them to face, preferably not from a noose rope. When those're down, maybe one last extra one to go. Himself.

There were settlers about the wagons and up on the rock mound, but out of wary habit, it was the blue-gray sheen of a moving rifle barrel that caught his eye. Before he could identify it fully, something stabbed along his ribs; he heard a report from the hillside and saw a wisp of smoke up there. Slumping to his knees, a wave of blackness passed before his eyes and the whole world reeled, and he found himself lying on his side. He could feel the numbness fading, but the pain was only a shadow of reality.

People were gathering, nameless voices. Some man said, "Way he flopped, he's dead or close to it."

"Well, I ain't staying here waiting for him to croak off."

"Not in this voodoo place. I vote we move out now."

"Wyndam's kept his guns. Y'think. . . ?"

"Naw, he'll bleed out, come morning. T'hell with him. I don't care why he's back or fought here. When all's said'n done, he still knifed Brimstone."

Their images were as blurred as their voices, yet a narrow tunnel of vision remained acute. In his crumpled position, his view happened to be focused on the rock mound about where, he thought, the shot had come from. He searched the boulders and saw a man standing there with a rifle in hand. His eyes ached as he strained to identify him ... Yes. Otis Wyndam.

A swelling wave of darkness bore down on him. In its approach his strength deserted him and he sagged lower, tasting earth.

Then a black void engulfed him.

8

The sensation of being dragged through scrubby sage that snagged at his buckskin jacket, and of being slid as gently as possible down the eroded bank of a stream, where the next impressions that roused Skye Fargo.

"This ain't the road to hell." He heard himself chuckle wildly. "It's too hot down there for sage and sand . . ."

Oddly enough he heard a girl's voice accompanying his. "Hush now." Water, blessedly cool, touched his lips. A damp cloth tenderly swabbed his face of caked dirt and blood.

Slowly stirring, then he opened his eyes and gazed up at Miracle Blutcher. "You're a surprise, and damn welcome one," he said after grinning a moment, then tried to rise. "'You and the train still here, 'eh? Good. Wyndam is due a sendoff—ugh!" He lay back prone, his side lancing agony.

"You're going nowhere," Miracle ordered. "I'm not either, not by wagon. They left before dawn like the camp was haunted. Now, let's have a look."

Slow and easy they removed his jacket, but his shirt stuck to the wound's congealed blood. Miracle gingerly peeled the shirt up. "Not bad," she said as they eyed the long, ugly bullet furrow along his ribs.

"Needs cleaning." She handed him the rag. "Wash it with stream water. I'll be right back."

Fargo moved to a low rock at stream's edge and did as he was told. He would've anyway; the wound stung and hurt, but shouldn't incapacitate him unless it became poisoned. Still, that could well prove unimportant. Wyndam and his train had swiped his horse, weapons, and personals, and abandoned him to the Northern Paiutes. The settlers thought they'd cause to leave him—but surely they wouldn't have thrown out Miracle.

He could not understand Miracle. He understood Julia Driscoll, and her fast jump aboard the wagon-train bandwagon against him. But Miracle was an opposite sort, drawn to outcast, offbeat trouble. Well, she got it. She was alone in a wilderness with a man lacking supplies or weapons, facing scalping or a flint arrow in the back. He would not ask her why she chose it. The answer might mean more trouble, and they needed luck, lots of luck.

"It'd be luck if she managed to filch a horse," Fargo murmured.

He heard the crisp sound of Mircale's ankle boots approaching the stream, and it was his answer. She had quit the train on foot. Pulling a ragged breath into his lungs, Fargo began calculating the miles to anywhere.

Miracle was wearing another laundry-boiled dress, looking to have been cut from the same bolt of cloth. At least she wouldn't be burdened with a woman's bulky clothes on the walk to come. In one hand she toted her father's antiquated Burnside carbine, powder horn, and shot pouch. In the other she carried a weighted flour sack. Crouching on a grassy strip, she opened the sack and took out a bottle of Dr. Seigismund's Magnetic Oil Tonic.

Fargo came over and Miracle told him, "Lie down here so I can see what I'm doing." Fargo lay down on his uninjured side; Miracle eyed the gash again and said, "Shut your eyes." And poured the tonic on the wound.

Fargo clenched his teeth. He'd had whiskey sloshed on wounds before, but nothing compared to this alcoholic acid that shot searing fire through his system. Cold sweat stood out on his body; he fisted his hands until his knuckles whitened and the tendons stood out all along his arm.

"That wasn't so bad, was it?" Miracle took her ripped dress out of the sack and tore it in strips, making a pad and bandage to bind his wound. "You'll be a little stiff, maybe. No great harm."

Fargo pulled himself upright and sat quite still, squeezing his eyes and blinking while Miracle emptied the sack. Bread, corn, jerked ox meat from a camp barbecue, and Brimstone's silvered quillon dagger in its sheath.

"Y'see? We won't become lizard-eaters." She laughed, handing him a chunk of bread and jerky strip, and then the dagger. "Wear it right, this time."

His smile ironic, Fargo accepted the knife, but his voice was grave. "We need to decide where to, start after we eat, and keep going. We're in central nowhere, and it's a long hike to anyplace. Seven wagon days to Fort Boise. Ahead is four, five days to the Ben Brown's Tavern settlement."

"What do you think?"

"Brown's settlement. It's easier, shorter, and on the trail west. With luck, we'll meet your train's other section that's a week behind, run by—"

"Tremayne, Lester Tremayne." Miracle nodded. "We go on. Some of Idaho was bare and bleak, but here there's water and game and no desert."

"Eastern Oregon is a high-plains desert, Miracle, snowing or baking and usually blowing. There're rivers, springs, and such, but the Paiutes lurk by them ambushing travelers, lost settlers, anyone. If we find sign of Paiutes, getting water may be a problem, and so may be game. Gunshots and cookfire smoke carry far and bring them hotfooting." Seeing her give a slight shudder, Fargo added, "We'll make it. We keep to cover on game paths, alert for sign. Maybe there won't be any. Watch for Tremayne's train. If it doesn't show, we'll get to Brown's in due course, that much nearer and well set to go on to Oregon City."

"I don't want to go there. Don't tell me you do, after what they did."

"I wouldn't give those knucklehead settlers the sweat off my ba—er, brow." Fargo's expression hardened; so did his tone. "But Wyndam has my horse and my weapons"—he patted his wounded side—"and I took something of his that I plan to return."

She sighed. "I'm so sick of trouble. Skye, don't go. There're other guns, other horses. You don't have to go."

"Yeah, I do. For the same reason you kill a rattlesnake slithering over your foot, 'cause if you put it off, you might not get another chance later on."

Soon they started out. Fargo struggled up the bank, refusing help, knowing the sooner he came to terms with his wound, the better he'd feel.

The stream flowed along a far rim of the bowl-shaped field, and from there they skirted the campsite across the westbound trail. Wyndam's hastily departing settlers had left the area in tidy ruin. The rock heap was neat but battle-scarred, and somewhere inconspicuous a mass grave would have been dug. Yet at the fringes were tattered remnants, damaged goods, other discards from the fight, including the charred shells of two burned-out wagons.

"One family bought Pa's wagon on credit," Miracle explained. "The other took Ike's wagon, but dumped his stuff for room. They got four kids."

Fargo chuckled. "Wait till the Paiutes scrounge up his tonic."

They hit the trail and walked along it until they found a game path into the flanking growth. From morning through the afternoon, as they followed that track and a series of others, the ground varied from rocky patches to soft mattings of soil and pine needles. Sunlight shone brighter where the trees grew more sparce in rocky earth, and then dimmed again when they entered stands rooted in fertile soil, so that the day alternated between noon and dark.

Fargo might've appreciated it more, perhaps, under different circumstances. But every folded wash and every murky thicket held potential danger for them, and the tricky shiftings between light and shadow made it all the more difficult. He found it harder to concentrate, too, his wound having dulled his sharp focus as well as slowing them down, especially during the morning. He'd walk until the pain in his ribs became intense, then rest and try to shake off the weakness. As the day progressed, his breaks became fewer and briefer, and his natural stamina began to outpace Miracle's.

Glancing at the girl every so often, Fargo could see that each step was becoming more of an effort, yet she was making a brave effort to match his own faltering stride. He figured they'd trudged ten slow miles already, and a few more at the most lay in front of them. He saw her face turned toward him, and she gestured at a flat boulder alongside the path.

Fargo shook his head. "We've got to keep moving," he said through gritted teeth. "Stop now, we'll knot up, cramp. Then we can't walk."

They slogged on, occasionally resting only for a moment when the weedy path rose steeply. The terrain grew rougher, higher, like overgrown steps to the southern flanks of the Lonepine and Dooley mountains. At times the trail led them dipping into a gully or gorge; other times they crossed meandering ledges and ridge-flanking benches. At sunset, they reached a small clearing that bordered a brush-clogged ravine. Other than the open rim line and the path, the clearing appeared entirely hemmed in by wild brambleberry thickets.

Miracle slumped down, too winded to go hunt with Fargo. Leaving her to rest, the Trailsman began prowling the nearby slopes and pockets for game. Throughout the day, it seemed, he'd heard grouse drumming in thickets, marmots barking from rocks, boar, antelope, beaver. Now . . . nothing. Not a peep, not a twitch. He continued diligently if irritably sweeping in a wide crescent that would bring him back to the brambleberry clearing—empty-handed, at this rate.

Stalking up yet another brushy grade, Fargo eased over the rounded crest of the hill and scanned the hollow below for black-tailed deer. At first he thought the dark objects scattered haphazardly about the copses were boulders; then abruptly he recognized them as rude brush hogans built by a band of Paiutes. With a sinking gauntness in his stomach, Fargo knew there was only one thing to be done: He must rouse Miracle and put enough distance between themselves and the Paiutes so that no roving warrior might find them.

Fargo hastened quietly back to the clearing, thankful that his hunt had been so poor. He hadn't shot or cooked any game. How much luckier can bad luck get? Arriving, he looked around to tell Miracle.

Miracle was gone.

He ran to the spot where he'd last seen her. Here, as elsewhere, the brambleberry thicket was impenetrable; no woman could have ever vanished through it. A fear it might be Paiutes kept him from shouting out her name, but he saw no fresh sign of them when he scouted the ground. He found her boot prints, then more farther on, toward the path. He began working along the path, and in his slow, noiseless scrutiny, he caught the sound of splashing water. A creek, he surmised, rippling along somewhere to his left.

Wrong, he realized after a closer listen. Natural splashing water has a rhythm; he was hearing the splashing of water by something else. He angled off the path through tangled brush, tracing the errant sounds past a placid creek that trickled into a copse. He shouldered forward, following the creek, and entered a shaded pocket with mossy earth fringing a sheltered pool.

Miracle was in the pool. Her clothing was piled beside its edge and she was blithely cavorting out in the clear water. When she caught sight of Fargo, she stopped swimming and began treading, a sassy look in her eyes.

There was a look of fury in Fargo's. "Get out of there!"

"Come and get me. I found it first, you could only find me."

"So will Paiutes!" Nervous, wary, Fargo was sliding the dagger from its belted sheath. "Didn't you see all these tracks around the pool?"

"From the animals? Yes, I hope a fawn'll come drink."

"They're moccasin prints. This is the local Indian water hole, you ninny! They'll kill you for being a white and then kill you worse all over again for contaminating their drinking supply. Now, out! Fast!"

"Well, you don't have to get mad at me," she pouted, paddling toward the edge. "How was I supposed to know. Anyway, I've been very quiet here."

But not quite quiet enough.

Nor was the Paiute quiet enough, a scuff of a foot behind Fargo warning him just in time. Swiveling, Fargo glimpsed a short, stocky figure leaping from a low, platformlike boulder just behind the screen of undergrowth. It gave the attacker the advantage of height and momentum, and he was using it well. Brownish tan of skin, black of hair and eyes, clad only in a breechclout, the Paiute had his mouth open to yell and his skinning knife clenched overhand to rip Fargo from belly to brisket.

Still pivoting aside, Fargo parried the slashing knife with a diagonal upthrust of his left forearm, while arcing his own blade high in a throat-slitting parabola. With the attacker's windpipe severed, the yell died unborn in a pink spray of blood. But Fargo took little notice, his attention focused on locating the next attacker, knowing from experience that Paiutes almost always worked in pairs.

The first attacker was tumbling limply against the bloody earth. Red droplets were raining from Fargo's knife as he heeled around, eyes darting. The second Paiute was suddenly before him, launching himself from around the near boulder with an ax-edged lance at ready. Again Fargo blocked with his left arm, but the Paiute avoided his dagger's stab. They struggled, neither backing off, yet gradually Fargo forced the Paiute to give ground.

The Paiute broke then and attacked desperately

with all the tricks he knew. Fargo parried, but one stroke slipped under his guard and raked the same ribs that had been shot. Twisting in agony, the Trailsman saw his chance and took it. The last of his strength drove his blade upward from his side, the point sliding to the grip between the Paiute's ribs.

For a long moment they clung together, breath rasping from them, their bodies straining. Then all strength seemed to leave the Paiute. His eyes closed slowly and an awful agony twisted across his face. His breath whistled out; he fell and lay still.

Fargo pressed flat against that low boulder, catching his breath and straining eyes and ears for sign of other attackers. Satisfied at last that the soft soughing was solely the sound of an evening breeze, he wiped his blade clean and returned it to its sheath on his belt while his gaze strayed over to Miracle.

Now that the grassy edge was safe again, Miracle was scampering out of the pool, her naked breasts taut, her loins glistening with beads of water. Eyeing her wriggle into her dress, Fargo thought this fight was Miracle's doing. She hadn't done it intentionally, but simply by being Miracle, just the way he'd feared since the first moment he saw her. Some girls just go through life attracting trouble the way flowers attract bees, and Fargo was facing another dose of her poison honey.

But now was no time for regrets or recriminations. There would be women wailing in the Paiute village, come morning, and there would be red wolves combing the hills seeking their revenge. This was Fargo's thought when he felt Miracle's hand on his arm.

"I'm sorry, I didn't think. I was so frightened!" She threw her arms around him and pressed tightly, warmly against him. "Are you hurt?"

"No." Fargo grinned wearily and moved from her

embrace. "But we'll both be Paiute bait by morning or before. This means we've got to keep moving, and moving fast. Drink now, we've got to slake up all the water we can."

Nothing had every tasted better to Fargo than the pool water. It was something to remember in the first frantic hours they fled. Through scratchy thickets, over mazes of timber, down dry rocky streambeds, up rocky hillsides where boots left no mark, he dragged the failing girl, sometimes carrying her. Striking northwestward through untracked wilderness, forgetting any notion of paralleling the trail for a while, they prayed for a delayed dawn that would add more miles behind them, so that some hound-nosed Paiute might not quickly pick up the faint traces they were leaving.

Daylight caught them on a timbered ridge where a rocky upthrust provided a sort of fort. Fargo elected to spend a few hours. Miracle sagged to the ground and fell asleep at once, but Fargo was too keyed up to do the same. His mind raced ahead, covering the days that lay before them. And he found them hell. They were burning up a lot of energy and would need food, the last of her flour sack of groceries had been eaten on the run last night. Meat roamed the area, but Fargo wouldn't dare fire the rifle until they were much farther away. Even now, marmots chattered at them from the rocks, so close, indeed, that Fargo tried to bag one by hurling rocks. Each pitch caused savage pain from his side, and his knitting wound upset the coordination of his throw. He had no luck. Reluctantly he woke the girl and they struck out again.

They had luck at midday, however. They found a deer carcass freshly slain by a questing cougar. They could not risk a fire, but gorged themselves on the raw meat and rested there until long cut strips of the flesh had dried. They moved on yet again, holding to the deeper timber lest some keen Paiute eyes be watching from the heights.

At sundown, Fargo left Miracle in a thick fir grove. He ranged far afield, returning in an hour with a fool hen he had knocked off a limb with a stick. It bulked small against their consuming hunger but it was food and they were grateful for the comfort of it, after Fargo had roasted it over a small blaze he dared to light.

When they had picked the bird clean, Miracle stood barefoot and stretched, her hands up under her hair, fluffing it. A girl like this one could drive a monk crazy, Fargo thought.

"I've covered our trail as well as I know," he told her, "and I think we can chance making this our camp for the night."

"And tomorrow?" she asked casually, beginning to undo her five big yellow buttons. "And the days after that?" she added, pulling the open front of her dress away from her skin, which was the color and texture of cream. "I'm so hot and the dress is so sticky after running so long. Ah, this is better." She sighed, completely unabashed, as if she and Fargo were longtime lovers, used to each other's undressing.

Fargo struggled to answer her question. "If we can get back near the trail, and do as well tomorrow and the next day as we have so far, two full days, maybe part of a third, should see us at Brown's settlement."

Strange lights glittered in her eyes. "We'll have to make the most of everything, won't we?" She leaned closer to Fargo, the top of her dress open and her slim hips undulating. "I'm twenty. I'm plenty old enough."

Fargo was growing aroused, but he was also growing tired of her flirting. He wondered how far he could get with her, or rather, how far she'd go for what she wanted of him. But eager as she might be, she evidently wanted him to be the first to act. So Fargo cupped her chin and kissed her.

She responded with enthusiasm, pressing her body against him, her arms circling his back and clinging for a long, burning moment. Then she stopped, breaking away, and faced him with eyes curiously tight at the corners, and waited, silent.

Fargo knew what for. Slowly he eased off her dress, and they slipped down on the springy mattress of needles. She hesitated, her eyes aglow with hidden fires. Then she pushed him slowly down until he was lying on his back, and she wouldn't let him do anything except receive her erotic caresses and fondle her large, firm breasts. They seemed like minor furnaces, all her passionate heat concentrating in her twin mounds and jutting nipples.

Fargo felt her body tremble, felt her weight. His readiness poked the crotch of his pants into a tent as she moved her lips and tasted his mouth and gave him her tongue, moaning with pleasure. Miracle was acting as if she were the man, the agressor. Fargo let her, enjoying her ardent advances as she kissed his neck and ears, while her hands dealt surely with the buttons of his fly. He raised his hips to allow her to remove his pants, but his shirt they left on because of his wound, though it began to ride up some.

Her lips, hot and moist, returned to lave fire on his lower abdomen, then tease lower, dipping to the insides of his thighs. She kissed him wetly, let her tongue drag on his skin, and then, when the tension was unbearable, she went down on him openmouthed, wide, wet, hot, swallowing all his girth. Fargo stiffened, tensing his muscles. Her tongue was rough, teasing his sensitivity. Then she went the length of him, down until her nose was against his groin, and back his entire length to repeat, and repeat again.

"You better quit before you blow a good thing," he panted.

Miracle laughed, low, liquid. She lay full-length on him, pushing his shaft into her softness, clinging to him, reaching between them for the hard member, guiding it into her.

It was a hard, quick union. Fargo lunged upward in sheer lust. Miracle moaned in her eagerness and pushed her pelvis downward in an arc to devour him, deep and hot and sliding in her belly. Faint cries of animal pleasure rose from her throat, her face contorting with desire, her mouth moving hungrily, her thighs rhythmically opening and closing around Fargo's pumping flesh. They were no longer aware of anything but the incredible sensations of the moment. Fargo quickened his upthrusts, searing and pulsating and deep, and the exquisite agony of nearing orgasm caused Miracle to thrash above him.

"Ohhhh . . ." she cried, moving faster and faster against him.

Fargo was aware only of the magnificent pressure building inside him and of the friction of their bodies as they heaved against each other. He came so violently that for an instant he was unaware that Miracle, too, was pounding, squeezing her inner muscles in tempo with his pulsing ejections. She spread her legs wide, pushing down with her hips, thighs, and buttocks, and held the last bits of joy there between her legs.

She purred then, a happy contented sound. After a long satiated moment, she slid off him and stretched out alongside, cuddling. She murmured, "I didn't join up with you for this. It's nice, but I don't want you to get the wrong idea."

Fargo had no ideas about anything right then. "Mmm."

"You never asked, but I imagine you wonder why I did."

"Mmm," Fargo repeated noncommittally.

"I've no family, nobody now. The women on the train never liked me much, always frowning at me like I want their stupid husbands. Then, when I tried to defend you and Ike wasn't there no more to back me, that was the capper. Called me an ingrate, and you my pa's killer, and . . . that sort of thing."

"I guess you know I didn't, huh?"

"Well, I know what Ike told me. He's the only one who befriended me. No, that's not quite it. Ike's the only one so old he was allowed to." She let out a giggle. "Oh, and Ike told me you were behind my stepmother belly-flopping buff n-naked in that m-mud bog—" It's as far as Miracle got; she started to chuckle, and her chuckling bubbled into laughter, spilling over. She rocked against Fargo, tears in her eyes. "Oh, Lord," she finally managed to gasp. "Oh, I shouldn't speak of the dead that way. A-anyway, I just felt I could believe Ike. And if he liked a guy and that guy had the guts to flat refuse Abigail, then I felt I could believe him, too."

"You're the one you should believe, and believe in."

"Thanks," Miracle said, and her eyes became wistful. A soft, faraway smile came to her lips. "This is my clean break, Skye, d'you see? I tried running away, but I'd always get brung back. They told me I was an abomination, needing to repent, and the worst sin of all is to have nothing to repent. And my demons had to get exorcized, and—" She stiffened, reverting to her puzzling self, as she'd been when Fargo first met her. "I talk too much, Skye. G'night."

She turned over, and Fargo covered her with his jacket against the quickening chill of the night.

Next morning, at first dawn, Fargo had some more luck. He beaned a jackrabbit behind the ear with a well-placed shot. Again they dared a small fire and ate hungrily of the stringy meat.

Much of the day they worked their way back to the vicinity of the Oregon Trail. From there they paralleled its course across the brushy country northwestward. They ate again from their slender stock of dried meat, and Fargo could see by Miracle's deep-sunk eyes that she was about at the end of her tether.

Yet, from the peaks that hazed the sky beyond them, Fargo estimated they were within a modest day's reach of Ben Brown's Tavern. When the following morning he pointed this out to Miracle, she studied the mountains and said, "Funny how it can cloud over up there and stay clear as a bell down here."

"Clouds get hung up on the peaks," Fargo replied.

The day was cool and clear; the sky promised to hold open for at least a day or two, he sensed, but he also realized that a storm was heading this way.

The pace was faster now, but nonetheless cautious. As the hours fled, Miracle found it more and more difficult to keep up, and they rested often. Gaunt, bearded, plainly showing the physical and mental strain they'd been under, Fargo did not object to the breaks. They ate, as they had all along, what the paths provided, and it hadn't been more than enough to keep them going. Roots, berries, bird eggs. Fargo knew they had to chance shooting, and he took the chance by firing at a wild turkey that sat in the low branches of a tree. They paused and stuffed themselves.

The break seemed to revive Miracle, but she soon flagged again. She was a brave girl, but her labored breath and grayness of face hinted at utter exhaustion no one meal or short rest could restore.

Then, gradually, the thing Fargo had been dreading happened. As they were crossing a relatively open patch, he saw the girl's feet fail to lift. She stumbled and only the quickness of his move saved her a fall. Arm around her waist, he supported her sagging weight.

Miracle raised her face, which silent tears had streaked. "Skye, I'm done," she said huskily. "I . . . I can't go on. Leave me . . ."

Laughter that held no mirth touched Fargo's lips. "You could have left me before we started," he grunted. "Put your arm around my neck. We're going to make that ridge up ahead. It'll be a nice place to watch for Paiutes coming from one direction and Tremayne's wagon train coming from the other."

The western sky was filled with crimson sunset as Fargo helped the girl up the last slanting rise of the ridge. He peered forward across the bluegrass landscape, his sudden shout making Miracle open eyes that deadened fatigue had closed.

Straight out there before them, eventide was gilding the stained wagon tilts of fourteen circled Conestogas and Pittsburgs.

"We made it," she whispered croakingly. "Let's hurry!"

"And I thought you were worn to a frazzle—" Fargo began, but he did not finish the sentence, for the girl's sudden spurt of energy had left her. He saw her tumble forward and lie still.

That last five hundred yards, Fargo carried Miracle. Alert guards stationed outside the ring of wagons saw them appear out of the evening, and blinked their eyes. And as they drew near, Fargo's battered, bruised face remained hard and resolute, but managed to find a smile someplace when it came time to greet the guards.

"This Lester Tremayne's outfit?"

"Right the first time," one of the bearded guards drawled, and then he got a glimpse of the girl's white face cradled against Fargo's chest. "Glory be to goshen," the guard exclaimed. "Iffen it ain't Miz Miracle Blutcher. Here, let me take her off your hands. My old woman will know just how to bring her 'round.'"

His arms were aching, his wounded side was igniting his ribs, but Fargo said stiffly, without stopping to analyze his reasons, "I'll carry her. You lead the way."

9

Cradling Miracle, Skye Fargo followed the guard into camp.

The travel-ragged wagons and gaunt stock, the weary faces of women preparing supper and men checking harnesses and ox yokes made this second section look very like the earlier half of Wyndam's train. In contrast to Wyndam himself, however, Lester Tremayne was a brawny, square-jawed ex-teamster of fifty, clad in homespun blue jeans. As he saw the new arrivals and came striding forward in his low-heeled wagoner boots, others began converging from all sides. The excited gabble of voices seemed to be enough to rouse Miracle, and back on her feet again, hand on Fargo's arm for support, she had a smile for Tremayne when he reached them.

"Our group got attacked," she explained after introductions, but skipped the details when Fargo gave her a warning nudge, and continued, "Anyway, we were separated and well, if it wasn't for Skye, I wouldn't be here now."

Tremayne's owlish eyes beneath shaggy brows studied them both, and his answering smile was hearty. "Yeah, you got the look o' a scout," he declared, extending a hand to Fargo. "Miz Blutcher's approval is enough for me."

Women with heaped plates of steaming dinner

and mugs of hot coffee were already about them. Hungry as he was, though, Fargo waved the food away and motioned to Tremayne. The train boss understood and followed him a short distance from the bunch gathering around Miracle.

When they were out of earshot, Fargo said, "I don't want to alarm your camp, but there's a band of Paiutes warpathing hereabouts."

"Must be, to've raided Wyndam's outfit."

"No, that was by a gang of whites disguised as Indians. A long story, we'll tell you later," Fargo hedged. "We ran into the Paiutes on the way here and had to kill a couple. I don't know how many are chasing our trail, but if they number enough, they're mad enough to strike."

"I'll redouble the cavvy guard and pass word to keep eyes peeled," Tremayne said thoughtfully, rubbing his jaw. "Brother, you must've been through this region before to've gotten through to us. Tell me about the trail up beyond Brown's Tavern."

"Right now, I can say it in one word: snow."

"You sure? Exceptin' a rain shower, the weather's been clear."

"Storms usually sweep in from the northeast, down along the Columbia Gorge, and I'm reading that one is brewing. My advice is to hole up at Brown's until the front passes."

Tremayne rubbed his jaw some more, lips tightening. "Your advice has merit," he allowed at last, "but we're moving on just the same. Just like we've been drivin' on Sundays even, to make time and p'raps catch up. Days mean too much to waste a one of 'em. Now, shall we go back?"

Right then and there Fargo became aware of two things: Lester Tremayne was a vain man, jealous of his authority as captain of this caravan; and he was also a stubborn man, one who would do things the way he saw fit, come hell or damnation.

Next morning broke gray and cold and did not improve greatly during the train's half-day journey to Ben Brown's Tavern. Fargo rode a hock-scarred dun gelding, and Miracle was on a liverish hammerhead mare; the best he could say for the borrowed horses was that they came with gear and four legs that reached the ground. Fargo also replaced his missing revolver with a well-abused Remington .44-40. It had a cracked walnut grip, the settler who'd sold it admitting he'd used it for a hammer, but at least it tossed lead in the general direction it was pointed. For how long was a touchy question.

Not a Paiute was spotted the entire time, and the wagon train arrived without incident. Brown's was sited on the Grande Ronde River, serving as a small crossroads junction with a handful of supply and repair facilities. The taproom in the tavern itself was a clearing house for news of Oregon, the Northwest, and the upper territories, and it was there that Tremayne found a message waiting from Otis Wyndam.

"He mentions the chance of snow, too," Tremayne remarked as he read Wyndam's note. "We're to follow him on General Stevens' route instead of risking the trail over Deadmans Pass. By looks of the little map he drew, the cutoff is about four miles on, and he writes he'll place an ox skull there as a marker so we won't miss it. The gent thinks of everything, don't he?"

"So it'd seem," Fargo replied grimly, and again drew Tremayne aside. "I hoped this wouldn't have come up," he began, and explained why the indicated cutoff or any other path south of the Columbia could not possibly be part of General Stevens' survey route.

"Wyndam showed me the charts before he left." Tremayne's lips curled a bit disdainfully. "I've every confidence in him, and in them. Besides, he's taking the same route, and it's not sensible to suppose he'd jeopardize his own life needlessly. You may be a top-notch trailsman, but I'm afraid you're not a good judge of character."

Fargo drew a breath, holding his tongue. Together, after breakfast, he and Miracle had jointly told Tremayne of the events and their suspicions concerning Wyndam's caravan, and Tremayne had laughed it all off.

"You've let an upsetting time color your thinking," he proclaimed. "I don't trust anyone blindly, but Otis Wyndam has been extremely fair in dealing with us, and I imagine you're both p'raps exaggerating a mite."

So Fargo had started out the day with a bad taste in his mouth, and Tremayne's talk now wasn't improving it any. He was unable to keep the hardness out of his lake-blue eyes as he stared at the wagon master.

"In a new country," he said deliberately, "a man learns as he goes along, if he's smart. I hope you'll be doing that."

The wagons moved on again after the barrels banded to their sides were replenished and the stock watered. The afternoon sky was covered by flat, mackerel-scaled clouds by the time a cry winged back along the line and the snakelike train rolled to a halt on the trail.

Fargo rode up to the group standing a few yards in advance of Tremayne's lead wagon. As he approached, he could see along the shoulder a squat cairn of stones topped by an ox skull. The bony snout of the skull pointed at the ruts of a wagon path angling from the trail and stretching due west toward the near-flanking Blue Mountains.

Grimly Fargo turned back to the excited bunch about the marker, and the very somberness of his lean visage quieted many of the settlers. He stopped in front of the wagon master. "Tremayne," the Trailsman said bluntly, "I'm asking you to hold the train right here until I can scout this cutoff and on along the trail. I won't be gone more than a couple of days—"

"Days! Days!" Tremayne's impatient voice cut Fargo short. "That's all I've heard from you. We haven't time to waste on your suspicions, any more'n we have waitin' for your storm that ain't stormin'!"

"This is just a lull. We're in for a bad blow."

"All the more reason not to wait! We've got to get across before the snow flies. Even hours count. Nope, I'll give no such permission as long as I'm captain. We roll in ten minutes into the cutoff, and you'll oblige me by rememberin' you're our guest and not a hired-on pilot or scout."

Fargo turned away, seething, and loped silently along the cutoff, seeking some sign to prove his point. Instead, there were the unmistakable impressions of wagon teams and wheels having recently traveled this way, and mixed with the crushed grass and chewed earth were dim grooves from passages long before.

Puzzled, he lifted his eyes to yonder lofty Blues. There did appear to be a gap between two of the peaks, he noticed, and from his vantage it looked as though a long canyon led up to it. But he had trapped in that craggy range and he knew how easily the appearance of terrain could change upon closer approach. If this was a trick by Wyndam, every man, woman, and child in the Tremayne outfit might well perish in the blind depths of some box canyon. As much as he smarted from Tremayne's rebuke, Fargo knew a momentary loss of pride was minor compared to the loss of an entire wagon train.

Presently, as the wagons were trundling across the corrugated flatland, Miracle trotted over to Fargo, her face wearing the strained look of worry. "I didn't say anything back at the trail, because I hoped I might be able to accomplish more by talking to Lester alone. But I couldn't. He only scoffs."

Fargo shook his head. "There're fools who'll listen and learn. And there's others who've got to butt their heads against a wall. I'm thinking Tremayne is the second kind."

That night the long wings of the deep canyon enclosed them on either side. A brawling stream edged the canyon bottom, and settlers buoyed by hope forgot the day's fatigue, catching strings of rainbow trout to fill their fry pans. They chattered brightly, as though the Willamette Valley was just over the next rise, and their spirits remained high the following dawn, when they started along a high, grassy shelf above the white-water stream.

The slope on their right was stippled with ponderosa and lodgepole pine, the trees ruffling in the chill wind that gusted from the north. The canyon rose steadily, growing narrower by the hour. Ox chains were groaning more frequently as the great beasts strained in their yokes.

Fargo rode on ahead. The canyon twisted and pinched to a bottleneck, but as he rounded a buttress of gray granite, the way leveled out ahead. Here at last, he thought, the stock would have a chance to rest weary legs. He continued on across the narrow flat, the tracks of the path clearly visible through the upland grass, leading into a gorge and a still-steeper climb.

"It's got me stumped," he muttered to himself.

Clouds obscured the sun, and the gorge was deep in shadow, its walls looming high and sheer to pine-crested rims. Behind him, Fargo could hear the wagons creaking into the meadow he had just quit. Tremayne was pushing the train, he thought, making good time despite the steep ascent of the path. Pressing onward, he rounded yet another bend, and then suddenly the gorge straightened like a rifle barrel in front of him.

Three hundred yards away lay the end of the path. A cliff wall, towering for many hundreds of feet, boxed the gorge there. And at its base rested the skeleton hulks of six weather-ravaged Conestogas.

For the space of a minute, surprise held Fargo. An initial thought struck that they were what remained of Wyndam's outfit, but as he spurred forward, the true picture of what he was seeing became readily apparent. The wagons had suffered through one winter, their crushed tilts and warped sideboards proof enough of what the weight of snow had done to them. Before them, the ground at the end of the box canyon showed recent marks of other wagons having been turned around. Fargo could pretty well surmise the rest.

As a land shark based in Oregon, Wyndam would make it his business to keep track of immigrant comings and goings. So of course he'd learned that an earlier party had taken this wrong turnoff and left the scar of their doomed track upon the land. He'd concocted fake maps and a plausible story, perhaps for a specific venture, but more likely as a fallback plan in case his usual swindle went haywire. Such as this time, when he'd sold too few acres to too many settlers. Cleverly, he had pulled out some wagons from his own caravan and brought them into this blind canyon to freshen the tracks already here. Then he had retraced his way to the trail and moved on ahead to join the bulk of his train. It had cost him three or four days' time, but his greed and fear must've made him consider it worthwhile to lure the Tremayne outfit into this detour.

However, nothing could keep them from turning back, just as Wyndam's wagons had done.

The thought was still in Fargo's mind when a rending, muffled detonation shivered the narrow canyon. The air was filled with an increasingly sullen rumble as of thunder, and the funnel of the canyon trembled as if shaken by a giant hand. Fargo reined his lunging, fear-maddened horse around and galloped back the way he had come, although the numb knowledge was spreading through him now that there was no need for hurry. No need at all. They wouldn't be returning to the trail. No, not one of Tremayne's fourteen wagons with their load of human freight.

It was as bad as he had guessed, Fargo saw as his horse carried him back to the narrow meadow. The line of wagons was at a dead stop, wreathed in choking dust and gritty debris. At their tail, a great, ragged scar rose where the high granite buttress had been before. Motionless, the settlers watched the last dribble of rocks trickle over its shattered crest, heaping higher the massive pile of boulders and fracture stone that blocked the canyon to a height of forty feet, and no telling to what depth. Atop the rim, Fargo discerned the black surface of a huge stone block, the telltale smear of a powder flash. Blasting powder had been poured into deep cracks up along the ridgeline and set off once the train had passed along underneath.

And up there too, he glimpsed, a figure made diminutive by distance sat regarding his handiwork.

Aboard the saddle on a splotched paint, Fargo recognized the Indian named Umpqua.

Cradled across the bows of his saddle, the steel of Brimstone's aged Burnside carbine felt cold against Fargo's palm. He lifted the weapon almost without conscious thought as he brought his horse to a halt. Steady in his seat, he swung the rifle to his shoulder, and the sights seemed to line themselves with automatic ease upon the figure on the rim. The wind was brisk, and Umpqua was beyond decent range, but there was a goodly charge of powder behind the ball in the barrel. Fargo caught the splotched paint across the sights and raised his aim slightly. His finger, as he squeezed the trigger, was cold as the granite that trapped their path of escape.

The carbine's report rang sharply through the canyon's silence, and Fargo saw that distant shape on the rimrock jerk stiffly. Umpqua seemed to sway as he wheeled the horse. Then he disappeared into the cloaking blanket of pines that mantled the high slope.

As Fargo lowered the carbine, he heard the shocked shouts of men who had been jaunty but an hour before. He heard the cries of women and the sobbing of children as he paced slowly nearer the disrupted train. Miracle came racing toward him, and when he dismounted, she pressed trembling against his chest. He gently eased her off. There were hostile eyes watching him, he could guess, and this was no time to create dissension. He and Tremayne and all the rest were going to have to pull together in the same yoke now.

Across the girl's shoulder, he saw Tremayne break from the huddle of settlers about the wagons and strike hurriedly toward them. Braced for trouble with the wagon boss, Fargo was surprised at Tremayne's appearance as he stopped before them, his face gray as the granite barrier, his eyes clouded with misery.

"Fargo," he said raggedly, "'I've been an idiot for not listening to you. A damned idiot. But I won't be one any longer. I'm turning my authority as train captain over to you."

It took a good man to admit error, Fargo knew, but he also realized that if he accepted the offer, Tremayne wouldn't be worth a hoot from here on in. Tremayne's courage and ready acceptance by the others would bolster morale and unite the train, and that meant more than anything else right now.

"I wouldn't take your command on a platter," Fargo replied, grinning. "You've had guts enough to bring this outfit nigh to three thousand miles, and folding now isn't going to help get us out of this jackpot. We're in it together and we'll lick it together."

A deep breath stirred Tremayne. "Fargo— Skye, perhaps I'll be giving orders to the rest of the company, but here on in, I'll be taking mine from you and—"

He was interrupted by a cry. From the tag end of the caravan nearest the slide, a voice wailed thin and full of fear. "The creek's rising! It's dammed up. We'll drown like rats in here!"

Fargo glanced at Miracle. "Quick, get back there and give those folks a smile and tell them nobody's going to drown. We can pull our wagons into the boxed end above the slide line if we have to. Tell 'em Tremayne said so."

He watched the girl hurry away as Tremayne said somberly, "If we're forced to do that, not a one of us will ever leave this canyon alive. Winter isn't far away, and we haven't provisions enough to last out the month."

Fargo was as well aware of that as Tremayne. The

image of those pitiful shells of once proud Conestogas at the end of the canyon came to his mind. That was what the Tremayne outfit would resemble next spring, if the coming snows caught them here now.

"There're six wagons at the boxed end," he said as much to himself as to Tremayne. "They were stupid to've driven that far in. The cliffs back there must be upward of a thousand feet high." Thoughtfully he scanned the northern wall of the gorge. "Here they're not over a hundred. There's enough slant to them so a man might climb to the rim."

"But damn it all, women and children and stock could never make it," Tremayne objected hoarsely. "Skye, with that water rising, we've got to do something, and do it fast. If we're pushed back, we're lost."

Fargo nodded. He studied the northern escarpment again, then turned his eyes down-canyon. Already the brawling stream had widened perceptibly. By morning or before, this meadow would be awash.

"We've got tonight . . ." he murmured to himself, and then his eyes sparked as they found the captain. "Tremayne, there's a way we can get out of here—women, wagons, stock and all."

Tremayne's tense face showed surprise. "How?"

"Ropes! Every wagon has got rope in it. Light or strong, it doesn't matter, we'll use each for what it'll hold. C'mon, this is for everyone to hear."

Five minutes later, Fargo was staring into a sea of anxious faces as he explained, "We'll need men to cut wood for bonfires, others to empty and dismantle the wagons. Bulldoggers, too, to hog-tie oxen and mules. I'm leaving the organizing of crews to you, Tremayne. I'll take ten of the toughest up top with me to haul up the wagons and supplies as they're hitched into slings down here. The kids can help keep the blazes going for light. And some of you women start cooking up grub. We're going to need hot food and coffee to keep this job going. But we can swing it."

"Swing it or go down fightin'," Tremayne shouted, and his booming, infectious laugh was like a pledge that no settler would die in this trap.

Fires at top and bottom burned the short night hours away. Logs set to keep ropes from chafing had long since been worn smooth. Pulleys howled as men bent their backs to raise heavy Conestoga wagons. It was a monstrous task, a red nightmare fought against creeping time. Fargo found himself everywhere, a thousand details requiring his attention. And ever below them was the widening black mirror of that rising stream.

The paltry moon flickered through sweeping clouds, and the night wind had a frosty bite as it swirled down from timbered heights. Fargo ordered each wagon and its load bunched to simplify the process of assembling them in the morning. Ten were up when the rising water snuffed one of the great bonfires illuminating the meadow below. Fargo saw the flames dwindle like a giant candle burning to the end of its wick, and poised on the rim, he bellowed down to those fighting folk in the meadow, "Abandon the rest of the wagons! Get up a few more slings of food and clothes. Shoot the stock we haven't saved. Then make ready to ride the slings yourselves."

Somberly he regarded the death canyon below. In some faroff camp on the Oregon Trail, Otis Wyndam would be chuckling. But maybe not so far off at that, considering the delay his trap had caused him; and maybe he wouldn't be chuckling long, considering they and the storm were heading his way.

Weary to the point of numbness, Fargo still could

not rest as he saw the exhausted settlers sprawl on the pine needles beneath the pines. Many had scrapes and bruises from the night's ordeal, and a few had more serious sprains or cuts, but none had been lost or disabled. Four wagons had been abandoned. On the morrow trout would be swimming through their tilts. He turned then, seeing Miracle approach with a blanket in her arms.

"Skye," she said imploringly, "put this around you and go lie down. You can't keep going forever, and we'll need you more tomorrow than we do now."

"In a while."

"This minute. Or I'll call Lester to sit on you." She led him into the surrounding grove, away from any interruptions by others, and made him roll up in the blanket underneath a bowerlike hedge. It didn't take much persuading, actually, and he began dozing off the instant he settled down.

Then a warm body snuggled in alongside, sharing the blanket. Miracle gave him a kiss, affectionate at first, lazy and teasing. Then it changed, and a smoldering passion seemed to catch fire in her, and her hands began wandering. Fargo felt that he needed her like he needed a bad case of poison ivy. He was hardly in any condition to promote a great, lathering romp, but he supposed that was what made men different from women. When a woman's ready, a man will somehow rise to the occasion.

He couldn't refuse. He was firm about what he could do, however, and they wound up getting something straight between them. . . .

10

Dawn, and its problems, came before Fargo realized he had been asleep. He met Tremayne at the breakfast fire where women were preparing a community meal, and drew the captain aside.

"Lester, while you get the wagons and company assembled, I'll tackle scouting a route for us. I've a couple of ideas on that. We're too high now to try backtracking to Brown's, but if we head west, sooner or later we're bound to reach the Willamette Valley. May take us weeks. We might hit canyons where we'll have to dismantle and lower the wagons, haul 'em up the other side like we've done here. It'd be a long, tough journey."

"And your other plan?" Tremayne asked.

"We work north, more or less along the spine of hills, until we intersect the trail. I don't know if it'd be any easier, but it would be shorter. And there's the chance that at higher elevations, the coming storm will be too cold to snow, at least for a while. And like you told me, even hours count."

"It'd be a gamble," Tremayne observed. "Either way we're gambling. I'll take a flyer on the big one with you. Start blazin' your trail, mister!"

A chilly wind that brought its definite threat of winter whipped Fargo as he rode along ridges of mountain pines. Short ax gripped in his left hand, he estimated the distance between trees, seeking the easiest path for the Conestogas to follow. For quite a long ways the trail was open. Then a tangle of windfall trees, like a gigantic pile of jackstraws, blocked his progress. He detoured to the left. Here the slope grew dangerously slant, but with ropes snubbed about trees, the wagons could be held and inched on forward. Forward they must go, with an absolute minimum of time spent on roadbuilding.

When Fargo looked upward and off beyond, he seemed surrounded by looming ice-capped spires and crags banking away against the bleak sky. The storm was still holding off, at least up here; it was appearing increasingly gray and diffused down in the winding ravines and rubble-strewn chasms, as if chill mists were gathering to crystallize into snow. Speed was the only thing that would aid them now. Fleetingly, Fargo thought of Otis Wyndam and his caravan, whose delayed progress would place it around the 3800-foot-high Deadmans Pass, not much better and perhaps even worse off than they were.

Then he forced his attention back to the task at hand. After that it was twist and turn and climb, blaze trees and hike some more. He crossed a bald saddle, dropped into a clefted gap, and forded a creek running shallow with a thin-ice overlay that his horse's hooves cracked into diamond-sparkling splinters. He continued until late afternoon, when he breached one last crest before returning. On the northern slope the windswept side was more barren; when he looked back at the timber behind, he marked the contrast between the two sides.

From the crest he could see the country ahead, a vista of bends and rough breaks. Yet after considering ways and means, he mentally staked out a course from off the ridge, down between the slab walls of a gorge. The walls restricted his view, but beyond the gorge he could glimpse a wide plateau. A plateau that stretched north and westward as far as he could see.

Fargo relaxed with a sigh of relief. There was plenty of unknown territory down that way, but generally it appeared as though the train might be able to make at least the vague, murky end of the plateau. He bundled tighter in his buckskin jacket. The sky was darkening and the temperature was plunging as he started back.

The twinkle of campfires led Fargo to the wagon camp long after cold dark had closed in the mountains. The assembled settlers listened eagerly to his report, renewed hope supplanting their horrified despair of the previous day.

"This'll be a long, grueling trek," he cautioned in conclusion. "We'll need a hard two days to reach the crest, I figure, and how far we'll have to travel the plateau after that is anyone's guess. But there's a fair chance the plateau can drop us within striking distance of the Oregon Trail. If it does, my hunch is we'll come out twenty or so miles beyond Deadmans Pass, somewhere near the Umatilla River."

It took every minute of two days to reach the crest. Two days that brought sudden winter, ice, and frost on the slopes. The arctic blast split hollowed rocks, burst the staves of full barrels, and held the snow clouds massing low in the northeast. Two days that the dismal sky was like an oppressive threat driving them on with desperation. Two days that saw another wagon abandoned, when animals grown gaunt from insufficient feed were unable to pull the Conestoga a foot farther.

"We'll use the yoke for replacements," Fargo told

Tremayne. "Maybe the oxen will get some meat on their bones without a wagon to haul."

Strain was showing on everyone now, and Fargo saw eyes turn anxious whenever their faces craned toward the sky. It was the tail of the evening when the wagons circled on the crest. Stock so gaunt their bones were almost breaking skin halted in their tracks and pawed the frozen ground for graze.

Aside, where they could converse privately, Fargo spoke earnestly to the wagon master. "We may not like to, but we should rest the stock here a day or so, or we're liable to never make the trail."

"Yes, I had the same thought," Tremayne replied, and then blinked, something having fallen in his eye. He daubed it with his fist, and both men glimpsed a glistening fleck of white ... then more fluttered down. They stared somberly at each other while hearing a clamor over at the campfire.

"Snow!"

Fargo and Tremayne hurried to the firelit circle, Tremayne waving his arms for attention. "Calm down! We've got better things to do than booger at a few snowflakes. For starters, dump everything out of your wagons except food and blankets. The oxen just ain't up to luggin' your paraphernalia through snow."

"We also need to feed them and the other stock," Fargo added. "Me and your captain figured to lay over and fatten the teams here, but that doesn't look possible now. So those who aren't emptying the wagons, get out your knives and start cutting grass. Pack the wagons with every danged ounce they'll hold. Keep our stock strong, and we'll pull through. Starve them, and we'll starve."

A light dusting continued throughout the night, and by dawn the snow was inches deep. Protesting oxen broke the wagons in motion again, the white blanket crackling beneath iron-shod wheels, leaving a lacy pattern behind the Conestogas.

Fargo rode in front, hunting the smoothest path for the wagons to follow, and for a while he was joined by Miracle. "If this cold snap holds," he told her, "we won't get any more snow. But if it warms up, look out for trouble."

Miracle nodded. "Y'know, I can't help wondering how Wyndam's train is faring. Where they are, if the snow is worse, that sort of thing."

"Well, one thing is certain: Wyndam wants that strongbox money. It belongs to all the settlers in both sections, but he figures Tremayne's outfit is a goner, and plans to fleece his flock out of it all by hook or crook, mainly crook. So you can bet that he'll push through if he can."

"I suppose we won't find out until we reach the Willamette Valley. But it would be funny, wouldn't it, to meet up with him on the road down."

"Wyndam would die laughing."

At their midmorning break, Fargo offered to scout ahead to try to cut the trail, but Tremayne vetoed the notion. "We lose you, Skye, and none of us will make it. If the storm breaks while you're gone, you'd never find your way back. No, we've got to hang and rattle together, mister!"

During early afternoon, the sky grew darker. The air was quite dry but had a softer, warmer feel somehow, and foggy clouds were so low that Fargo could see no great distance at all. They were descending gradually in a north-by-northwesterly line, into the teeth of a northern wind that buffeted like the drum of a stampede, stinging faces, whipping clothes and flapping wagon tilts.

Fargo reined close to Tremayne and leaned half

out of the saddle to yell directly at the wagon master. "Hitch ropes from tongue to tailgate of each wagon, and another line from your lead wagon to the cantles of our saddles."

"What?"

Fargo stretched and yelled into Tremayne's ear, repeating his suggestion and adding, "We'll keep pushing on, snow or no damned snow, and we won't need to worry about wagons getting lost or out of line."

Tremayne nodded his understanding and started ordering it done.

The first flurry hit them before the job was finished. Looking across his shoulder at the swirling flakes, Fargo watched men and women struggling to string ropes between the wagons as they kept moving. By the time Tremayne was back beside him with lines to hitch to their own saddles, the snow was coming down in steady sheets, and the lead wagon fifty feet behind was a dim blur.

Through the muffler wrapped about his face, Tremayne mocked himself in a loud voice, "Days! Days! I ain't waiting any longer for your storm, Skye."

Fargo grinned sardonically, but did not speak. No words were needed. Both knew that if they didn't reach the trail before the day was out, they would never make it alive. Five feet of snow would blanket this plateau by morning, and weary oxen could not smash their way through drifts that high.

Only the lines strung between the wagons were keeping some from straying now, Fargo knew, as he paced blindly head-on into the blizzard. The feel of wind and snow against his face helped guide him. The front of the storm was marching from the north-northeast, so by keeping the gusts coming from a quartering direction, he was reasonably sure they were still headed on course.

The horse stumbled beneath him, then tipped forward. They were at the head of a sharp decline. Pines reared like white phantoms on either side, and Fargo gritted his teeth, nodded to Tremayne, and let the wagons come on. The downhill grade itself was not his main worry, for now they could pull through drifts that would halt a wagon on the level. He couldn't see what lay at the bottom of this slope, and for all he could tell, the slope ended at the rim of a bottomless abyss.

It turned out that another icy stretch lay ahead, leveling out across a wide, naked flat. The wind rolled in with a long reach and thus enough power to clear the snow from the ground. It very near cleared the wagon train off as well. At the far end, the flat slanted downward into a thick stand of timber, and here the wind dropped sharply as the forest took the brunt of it, the new snow falling almost straight down.

Fargo pulled his horse alongside Tremayne. "Once you're through the trees, bear hard left."

"Yeah? Why?"

"That's the trail, that's why!" Fargo gave a laugh of hearty relief. "I recollect there's a road ranch about two miles farther on. It's the closest shelter, if the wind hasn't blown it off the landscape."

Within the hour they were turning onto the Oregon Trail. It was fortunate that its route here was well-defined by its timber borders, because otherwise it looked like every other broad, open expanse under snow. As it was, about all Fargo could see on either side was the vague shadows of trees being bent by the wind; the storm was a swirling fury that all but blinded him as he and the others progressed at a snail's pace through the howling blizzard.

The two miles were the longest damn two miles ever traveled.

Eventually, though, the trail curved around a large boulder, and yellow speckles of lamplit windows could be glimpsed through the gale. They came from the road ranch, Fargo felt sure. He couldn't recall it having a name, and only remembered it because of the peculiar ranch house, which consisted of three blocky log cabins crammed up into one another, with a squat common chimney rising up at the meeting of their roofs. One side cabin was the owners' living quarters; the other side was a sort of dormitory with built-in bunks; and in between was a saloon and dining hall with a rear exit to an outhouse, stable barn, and corrals.

As they approached, Fargo could see the snow piling up against the sides of the ranch house. Beyond, in the broad yard that extended back to the stable barn, he spotted something loom out of the white maelstrom. It looked like the high, ghostly tilt of a Conestoga, and then it was gone in the scud. He battered his way closer, peering, and saw the wagon again with another in front of it, then another . . . Pulse quickening, he guided the creeping wagons of Tremayne's outfit around the corner and down the yard toward the barn and corrals. He had to anyway, so the stock could be properly tended, but on the way he eyed the long line of unhitched Conestogas and Pittsburgs that were parked along there, stranded as they were by the rampaging blizzard.

He heard Tremayne cry something that sounded like "Wyndam!"

Wyndam? Yes, this was his caravan. Fargo recognized Pickadilly Ike's smallish Murphy wagon nestled in with the prairie schooners. Gloved hand brushing back to his belted knife sheath, he drew out the dagger from beneath the many layers of shirts lent him by the settlers, and slashed the rope binding him to the lead wagon behind him.

Careful because of the ice under hoof, Fargo rode into the barn. After taking care of his horse, cleaning the packed snow from its nostrils, he left to take care of Wyndam. By then Tremayne's outfit had rolled to a halt, the settlers hastily unyoking, Tremayne calling to Fargo to wait.

Motioning instead for them to hurry and follow, Fargo fought the breasting force of the storm around to the front porch and entered the saloon door.

11

Inside, the one rough-hewn room of the tavern was poorly lit by sooted kerosene lamps. It had a dank smell of wet clothes and close, fire-heated air; the atmosphere was slightly steamy. Hardly a wonder, for it was swamped with refugees from the snowstorm.

Someone shouted testily, "Shut the goddamned door!"

Fargo put his weight against the door and pushed it closed against the wind. Casually, then, he removed gloves, undid his jacket, tucked back some of the numerous shirts, and hitched his shell belt so the holstered revolver rode easier. All the while he was scanning the room, but saw no sign of Wyndam.

"Christ a'mighty," someone exclaimed. "It's that Fargo maverick!"

A silence cut through the crowd of Wyndam's settlers like an abruptly drawn breath. Fargo ignored it, striding toward the bar. He was just leaning on the counter when the door opened again, and peripherally he glimpsed Tremayne and a few men of his outfit walk in. Their appearance shattered the hushed silence, a startled clamor erupting about the room.

"Glory be! Lester! How in tunket did you get here?"

There was bite to Tremayne's voice. "Why? Ain't I supposed to?"

"We dunno! Wyndam's been opinin' your bunch mightn't make it."

"Maybe Wyndam is the one who won't be seein' the Willamette, chums. Gang around, we've got some interesting news for y'all . . ."

Apparently indifferent to the hullabaloo, the bartender and a patron were discussing supper when Fargo leaned in. "I saw the meat slab hanging in your cooler," the man was saying. "C'mon, it's been a week since I ate any bacon."

"Pardon," Fargo said politely. "Where's Otis Wyndam?"

The bartender said placidly, "Do we have a Mr. Wyndam in our party? I don't observe him among the convention assembled."

"In the back room, playing poker," the patron explained. "He's the gentleman you lent the deck of shaved cards. Now, about my bacon."

"Down the rear hall, last door on your right," the bartender told Fargo, then turned back to the patron. "It ain't bacon, Ralph. It's dog."

"Dog!"

Leaving the patron lividly cussing the bartender, Fargo headed for the rear hall, a shadowy corridor that led to the back exit. As he approached the last right-hand door and saw it closed, he tried the knob. It was unlocked.

Without a pause Fargo stepped into the room.

Light glowed smokily from three candles flickering in a cluster on a wooden table. The room itself was small, square, its only exit the doorway behind him, Fargo saw with his first sweeping gaze; around the table three men were seated playing cards, and a fourth player's chair was empty, his cards facedown on the table. Of the three men, one was young, lanky, and badly scarred. The other two were Arvin and Umpqua, and they were all loaded with weapons.

Fargo took time to kick the door shut behind him, and even that slight delay was costly. The lanky kid smelled trouble and acted without speaking. His pistol was drawn and firing as Fargo lunged desperately to one side and fired back. Through the bright muzzle flashes and ear-deafening reports, Fargo felt the burn of a bullet against his already wounded side. He was pulling the trigger again, still moving in the lunge, when Arvin slapped all three candles off the table, and the low-roofed room was drowned in utter blackness.

"Damn you, Fargo," the heavy bellow of Arvin rang out. The table crashed over, and from behind its cover, Arvin triggered his revolver.

Fargo was dodging back the other way as Arvin's pistol spat fire. Umpqua shot then, almost the same instant the lanky man's gun spoke a third time. Fargo shot at Umpqua's muzzle flash and kept moving fast along the floor, and when all three men shot wildly at him, they missed.

Men in the passage jerked the door open. "What's wrong?"

The lanky man fired at the doorway. A man yelped with pain and jerked away, slamming the door closed. But for that instant, Fargo had been caught outlined by the feeble light from the hallway, and Arvin's gun opened fire at the spot where Fargo had been. Three shots as fast as the old man could pull the trigger. One of them drove splinters of wooden flooring into Fargo's face. He hammered another shot, trying to conserve his dwindling load of bullets, and kept on going back across the room. Men cursed and shouted outside the door.

Ears could hear little, but the cry that came through the powder reek was audible. "Arvin! He hit me!"

Arvin did not answer.

"Arvin?"

Fargo fired at the voice and jumped to one side by the door. He stood there motionless, cocked revolver in one hand, dagger in the other. There was no other way out of the room. They would have to pass him, and he knew why they were silent. Somewhere in the blackness they were waiting, or they were slipping toward the door.

He heard a faint scuffing to his right and swung that way, barely in time. The man came with a desperate rush, and was almost to the door when Fargo shot at the sound. Then a viciously swung chair slammed into his arm and shoulder and drove him back against the wall.

The rip of a knife blade went through the layers of shirts and nicked his shoulder. The gun misfired as he lunged over against the man's rush, and it was then, as the chair dropped beside him, that he realized he was struggling against Umpqua. He struck out with his knife hand and blocked another vicious stab. No longer trusting the gun to fire, he clubbed the heavy barrel at the spot where Umpqua's face should be. The Indian stumbled against him, and when Fargo pistol-whipped again, Umpqua went down heavily.

Taming his ragged breath, Fargo took his post beside the door again. In the reeking quiet of the room, he said, "I'm waiting, Arvin."

A quavery voice spoke in the darkness, "Don't shoot no more! I'm strikin' a light!"

A match sparked. By its brief sputtering flare, Arvin relit a candle with trembling hands. Fargo kept his useless revolver in his fist as his eyes, like softly glowing coals, surveyed the carnage. Smoke hung heavy in the room, a fuming pall helping to shroud the bullet-pocked wood and crimson splatters of blood. Umpqua and the lanky man were dead. Arvin sat weakly against the wall, clasping his lead-shattered arm.

"Up." Fargo nudged Arvin with his boot. "Where's Wyndam?"

"Went out to piss a minute afore you came in," Arvin panted, laboring to his feet. "Go get him. Leave me alone, you ain't got nothin' on me."

Fargo prodded Arvin doorward, grinning mirthlessly. "You're walking into the saloon and telling all those nice settlers how you're fixing to bilk them. Faking maps, phony deeds, whatever you and Wyndam have been conniving."

"'I ain't—"

"Okay, we stay. Blow out the candle."

Arvin blanched and stumbled out the door. "To hell with Otis and his fancy notions of easy money. I'll tell 'em true!"

On the way up the hall, Fargo glanced back at the rear exit. It was ajar, spilling a shaft of lamplight into the dark backyard area, and he could see snow coming down, fairly lightly now, in the night. Ahead, there was an abrupt hush in the crowded saloon; boots shuffled, forming an aisle, and the bartender stood frowning behind the counter, scratching his beard.

"For a minute there," he said, "it sounded like an engine crew beating on a steam boiler with twelve-pound sledges. Did you have a reason for all that, or was time just hanging heavy on your hands?"

"I had reason," Fargo said, and to help mollify any vengeful kin of the lanky man, he added, "Afraid I don't know who one of the guys in there was. I'm sure he was honest and industrious, and will be sorely missed. But he made his choices and there was really nothing I could do to avoid it." He gazed around then with a thin, steely grin. "Meet Arvin, folks. He's all set to claim your land, once you pay Wyndam. Tell 'em, Arvin."

"Yep," Arvin snuffled, "d-don't string me up, I'm fessing all. And I honestly own some prime bottom land I'd sell cheap if it'd help . . ."

Once uncorked, Arvin jabbered like a politico, mostly confirming what Fargo already knew and adding minor details but no startling revelations. Fargo parted early from the throng, stepping outside and back around to the parked Conestogas. The force of the snowstorm had noticeably slackened as the front passed on southward, and now it seemed to be subsiding further, although the temperature held to a low point.

With numbed hands, Fargo ransacked Wyndam's wagon for his Colt revolver, Sharps, and saddlebags with their winnings from Fat Dan Tobin's casino. It didn't take long, Wyndam having taken no precaution to hide them, having never thought he'd need to. Fargo checked his firearms, was pleased to find that his revolver was loaded and capped, and was climbing down out of the wagon when Lester Tremayne approached, watching the determination in Fargo's face.

"Dammit, I wish I know how you can stay so damned stony."

"Old habit," Fargo said. "Never let the other fellow know how scared you are." He smiled. "Anyway, I hope Wyndam's here. Let's find his tracks."

Tremayne said worriedly, "Maybe we ought to just let him go."

"Been talking to Miracle, eh? Well, if Wyndam

gets away scot-free, he'll be back to cheat or kill others. And your money will have helped grease it."

They were walking now around the rear of the ranch house. A quick tour around the outhouse and rear door picked up where someone with shoes like Wyndam's had made a trip to the outhouse, come back to a point perhaps five feet from the rear door, and then turned directly toward the barn and corrals.

Fargo stared thoughtfully. "Wyndam's hiding in the stable."

"Or stole a horse and escaped," Tremayne said, glancing nervously.

"Way I read it, Wyndam was returning when he hears gunfire and bolts. He doesn't know what's wrong, or what if anything it'll have to do with him," Fargo explained as they followed his tracks. "So he wouldn't make a break for it, not in this weather if he can avoid it. He'd lie low, ready to play it however it goes."

"Well," Tremayne said, "all right." They moved through the snow until they reached the trampled area around the barn and corrals, and he was plainly worried. "If you're right, Skye, this is a good spot for him to cut us down."

Fargo dumped his bags and gave him the Sharps. "Cover me, then."

"Wait a minute," Tremayne said, but by then Fargo was gone, sprinting across the open ground to the front corner of the barn. Horses milled around in the corral and a farther pen contained mules. No unusual sounds pierced the stillness. Fargo waved to Tremayne, who darted forward with the Sharps in one fist, his own gun in the other, and reached the wall breathing fast.

Fargo said, "I'm going in. Cover me from here."

"Maybe we oughta both—"

"My way," Fargo murmured, and dived inside the barn.

Quietly, cautiously, Fargo eased deeper into the dim interior. He worked his way along the main aisle of stalls, avoiding an open area where feed bags were stacked, wondering if his fancy guesswork was a load of horse puckey.

A scratch of sound turned him.

A burst of noise rooted him. From the far murky depths of the barn, Otis Wyndam launched plunging straight at Fargo astride a galloping horse. Wyndam was leveling a Colt Dragoon revolver, thumb on hammer. The horse was a war-charging pinto with a shiny black coat, save for a unique white blaze from withers to coupling.

"I know that Ovaro," Fargo yelled. "That's *my* horse!"

His outraged shout was lost in the thunderous blast of Wyndam's Dragoon. The slug clipped his buckskin fringe, so close that it snapped Fargo from his startlement. Obviously Wyndam had counted on that shock, just as he counted on Fargo's reluctance to shoot his own pinto, to gain a vital edge. What he had not counted on was the difficulty of aiming accurately from aboard a racing horse. Fargo, deciding to gamble on it, stood his ground there in the middle of the aisle, taking careful aim at the oncoming horse and swaying rider. A second wild shot past his left ear brought a cold laugh from between his teeth.

He squeezed the trigger. Lead speared Wyndam in the breastbone and dumped him from the saddle. The unharmed Ovaro left him sprawled and twitching in the aisle while it swerved by Fargo and tore on outside. Let it, Fargo thought; it could do with a cooling off. He went after Wyndam.

Wyndam was not where he had fallen, much to Fargo's annoyance. He had been a hair off, his shot striking lethally, but not quite instantly fatal. Wyndam was staggering on saggy legs away from Fargo, down a side aisle toward the shelter of the stack of feed bags. He fell to one knee.

"Pack it in," Fargo called. "Rest easy, Wyndam, you're through."

Wyndam turned, glaring, his face slick with sweat and his eyes feverish with defiance. He had a tenacious hold on his revolver, and as he aimed it, his voice rose, rasping, reverberating in the barn. "I'm not done with this fight yet—or with you!" He triggered, his slug coming amazingly close.

Another bullet punched into Wyndam and ripped a moan from him. He flung himself to the ground and began crawling. Fargo sprinted to catch up, again yelling to surrender while Wyndam was just starting in along the edge of the feed bags. Wyndam rolled over and pointed his smoking Dragoon. Reluctantly Fargo shot again, but Wyndam was beyond feeling or caring anymore, existing solely on pure hatred as he vainly tried to line his next shot. He was struck twice by one slug, then, which bored through his arm and lodged in his lower gut. The revolver dropped from his hand, but he did not pick it up. He was intent only on reaching cover, his right leg hanging limp and useless as he dragged himself ahead. He died with his good knee crooked for the last shove that would have sent him all the way behind the bags.

Fargo went to make sure Wyndam finally expired, then started back toward the barn entrance. Rarely had he seen such adamant stamina, but it reminded him of an old adage he once heard: born killers require a lot of killing.

He stepped outside, seeing many of the settlers converging on the barn, waving, shouting his name. He also saw that the wind had died away and the snow quit falling, at least for the moment. On the far horizon, a clear patch of night sky was breaking through the cloud cover, and moonlight was turning the surrounding terrain into a spectral sculpture of shadow and silver.

It might just be a good day tomorrow.

If nothing else, it would be a new day.

LOOKING FORWARD!

**The following is the opening
section from the next novel in the exciting
Trailsman series from Signet:**

THE TRAILSMAN #67

MANITOBA MARAUDERS

---

*1861, at the foot of Turtle Mountain,
where the northland called Canada
was still a wild and unformed giant. . . .*

"How dare you come sneaking into my bedroom
at this hour of night?" the woman snapped at the big
man with the lake-blue eyes.

"I guess I got lost," Skye Fargo said.

"That's very unlikely," the woman sniffed.

"Then you must've invited me," Fargo said, and
watched righteous indignation flood Alma Dunlap's
face.

"I did no such thing," Alma snapped.

Fargo's smile was cheerfully affable. "The hell you

didn't, honey," he said. "You invited me the first day
we met a week ago and you've been doing it ever
since, and this morning made a point of telling me
your husband would be away for the night."

"That was just a passing remark and you imagined
all the other things," Alma Dunlap said.

"Bullshit, honey," Fargo said calmly. "And we both
know it."

"You're being rude as well."

"And honest," Fargo added as he let his gaze roam
over the woman, prominent cheekbones, dark-blue
eyes of held-back fire, dark-brown hair, full lips.
Alma was on the shady side of thirty-five, he estimated, but still a handsome woman even with the
added layer of fleshiness that covered her full, am-
ple figure and the deep breasts under the dark-red
nightdress. She still pulled righteous indignation
around her, he saw as she speared him with her
dark-blue eyes.

"Why would I make overtures to a hired hand?"
she pushed at him, and Fargo's eyes narrowed.

"Watch it, honey," he growled.

"All right, you're not a hired hand," she said.
"You're the Trailsman, the very best. But Charles
has contracted with you to break trail."

"He has."

"And Charles could buy and sell you a thousand
times," Alma pressed.

"He could."

"He's a very wealthy man."

"He is." Fargo nodded.

"He owns a coach line, a cattle ranch, a gold-mining operation, a haulage company, and a saw-mill. He's running for governor of the province and he preaches every Sunday he can at church," Alma continued.

"Maybe that explains it."

"Explains what?"

"Why you're so anxious to get laid. He hasn't the time or the energy left to do it," Fargo said.

"What a terrible thing to say, Mr. Fargo," Alma snapped indignantly.

"Sometimes it's one and the same," Fargo said.

"What is?"

"Terrible and true," he answered evenly.

"You'd best get out of here right now," Alma Dunlap said; she stood very straight and her deep breasts pressed hard against the cotton nightdress.

Fargo let himself study her for another long moment. There'd been no mistake in his coming to see her. Reading signs was part of him, his life's work, and he did it better than anyone else. Alma Dunlap had been giving him signs since the day he arrived to meet with her husband, quick glances and long, meaningful ones, each with their own unspoken message, the handshakes that always lingered too long, the brushing against him that was never entirely accidental. She'd been smoldering and sending out signals that were unmistakable, and now he found himself shrugging with surprise at her.

"You want to back out instead of back in, you go right ahead, honey. It's a woman's privilege to change her mind," he said, and turned toward the door of the bedroom. "But this is a first, I'll give you that much."

"First what?" Alma questioned.

"First time I've seen cold feet win out over a hot pussy," he said, and had one hand closed around the doorknob when he heard her voice break the silence.

"Wait," Alma called, and he paused to glance back at her, his hand still curled around the doorknob. "I don't want to see you go away unhappy," Alma said diffidently with a small lift of her shoulders.

Fargo drew his hand from the doorknob and kept the smile inside him. "That's nice," he said laconically. "Because I don't want to see you go away unsatisfied."

Alma's eyes narrowed a fraction and she turned to the lamp and lowered the flame to a dim glow. Fargo came to her and she faced him with the back of her legs against the big bed. Alma Dunlap's dark-blue eyes smoldered and her prominent cheekbones seemed to grow more so as a sudden flush rose up from her neck and flooded her face. She exuded a raw earthiness, and all protests and words were done with, her little charade pushed aside, he knew, and he'd not question any of it now. His hand came out, pulled at the drawstrings of the nightdress, and the garment came open, fell away further, and Alma's deep breasts pushed out, heavy, deep-cupped breasts, each tipped by a dark-pink nipple and a brownish areola. Alma shook her shoulders and the nightdress tumbled to the floor. She wore nothing under it, and Fargo took in a still-firm body, a very womanly, full-fleshed body. Alma had an extra layer of fat on her, but it lay evenly without bulging at the wrong places.

A convex belly pushed out between wide, strong, and well-covered hips, curved downward to a black triangle that echoed the fleshy earthiness that was Alma. She waited and Fargo undid his gun belt, pulled off clothes, and saw Alma's eyes grow wide as she took in the beauty of his muscled body. Her eyes moved downward and her lips fell open as she focused on the rising, thrusting magnificence of his maleness. Alma reached out, curled fingers around his smooth firmness, and a tiny gasp of pleasure fell from her parted lips. He came forward, pressed himself against her, and she held on to him as she fell backward across the bed. "Ah, good, yes, good," Alma murmured as his face pushed into the heavy breasts, moved back and forth between them, drew first one then the other full, very soft mound into his mouth.

Alma half-turned, first one way then the other, as she brought her heavy breasts up against his face, an almost smothering embrace of flesh. Her hand reached down again, searched for him, and she uttered another sharp gasp as she found him, closed her fingers over the pulsating warmth of him. She moved to press her rounded belly up against him, and her arms circled his neck. She pulled his mouth down on hers and her tongue probed wildly, pulled, sucked, demanded as her body demanded.

Fargo brought himself atop her and Alma's earthy fullness enveloped him, her soft, fleshy thighs lifting to come against his waist. "Give it to me, Fargo, now, oh, God, now," Alma breathed, and pushed upward, wide hips lifting, insisting, and he felt her hold him, push with one hand, try to pull him into her.

He twisted and came free of her grip and she gave a small cry of protest that instantly turned into a half-scream of pleasure as he came to the very tip of her lubricious portal, held there, and let the tingling sensation flow through him. Alma was ready, waiting warm wetness, and her breaths had become soft groaning sounds of entreaty. There was no vivid, wondrous discovery of passion with Alma Dunlap, no wild delight of youth. But all that she replaced with a raw, groaning hunger that held its own enveloping quality.

She pushed forward to take him in, but he stayed just against her and felt the fleshy thighs fall open for a moment, then come together to slap hard against his ribs. "Come to me, damn you, oh, Christ, come to me," Alma breathed fiercely, and when he slid forward, slowly at first, then with a harsh, deep thrust, Alma's groan seemed to tear from deep inside her someplace. Harsh, almost guttural sounds came from her with his every sliding motion, and her wide hips lifted to meet him each time. Fargo saw the heavy-cupped, white mounds bounce as Alma rose, pushed up, and fell back. He buried his face into their creamy softness. "Yes, that's it, that's it, oh, Christ, more, more," Alma groaned out as Fargo pushed hard into her and saw the almost triumphant smile that touched her lips as, eyes closed, she pushed hard against him. "Jesus, more, more, agh, agh . . . aaaahhhh," Alma breathed, her voice hardly more than a whisper.

He felt Alma Dunlap's warm thighs lift further, press against his ribs as she tried to take in even more of him, and suddenly the concave belly pressed its warmth against him with a series of fleshy slaps. Alma's waist drew in and out sharply and the groaning sounds of pleasure took on an even deeper tone. "Ah, ah . . . I'm . . . I'm . . . ah, I'm coming, Christ, I'm coming," she cried out, and her fleshy body seemed to bounce and jiggle and her scream was a deep wailing sound. She clutched him to her, held his face between the deep breasts until her cry slowly faded away and became a low, moaning sound that was almost a hissing rumble.

"Good, real good," Alma breathed as he finally drew from her and stretched out alongside her. She stayed on her back and let her breath return to normal; he caressed one deep, white mound with his face, and she made small, low sounds of delight. Finally she half-turned, rose on one elbow, and let the deep-cupped mounds brush against his chest, and he took in the full-fleshed handsomeness of her, everything a trifle heavy yet everything held firmly together. He glanced up to see her watching him with a smile of satisfaction that held an edge of triumph in it. His eyes narrowed and he sat up. "I'm wondering why all that protesting before," Fargo said.

"Maybe I wanted to see how you'd handle it," Alma said, and allowed a smug smile. Fargo nodded and tucked the reply away in a corner of his mind. "You enjoy staying, Fargo?" Alma asked almost coyly.

"I did," Fargo answered.

"Then you'll come back tomorrow night," Alma said. "Charles won't be back till the day after tomorrow," she added at his questioning glance.

"Was it that good or are you that hungry?" Fargo smiled.

"Both," Alma said. "And I believe in making the most of an opportunity. I expected you for a man who felt the same way."

"I do."

"Then I'll expect you tomorrow night. Same time."

Fargo's eyes narrowed again. "That sounds like an order," he commented.

"Sorry," Alma said quickly as she caught the warning in his tone. "Just anticipation," she added soothingly.

Fargo pondered for a moment. The cattle drive he'd just finished before coming here to meet Charles Dunlap had been long, hot, and hard. The pleasures of a warm woman were definitely in order, and Alma certainly filled that description.

"Tomorrow night," he said as he reached for trousers. He dressed and Alma watched appreciatively from the bed. She remained unmoving, nakedly taunting, her full figure its own sensuous earthiness. His eyes held on her when he finished dressing, and Alma's smile was slow.

"So I'll stay in your mind this way till tomorrow night," she said.

"You'll stay." Fargo nodded and closed the door behind him. He paused at the rear door of the house to peer into the night before quickly striding to the Ovaro. Climbing onto the striking horse with the jet-black fore and hindquarters and the white mid-section, he rode slowly west till he found a grove of balsams and bedded down for the night.

Alma had been pretty much what he'd expected, he mused as he lay awake, except for an edge of possessiveness to her that bothered him. He'd seen other women give lip service to their morality as they got ready to toss it aside. It was as though they needed to assuage their own consciences before enjoying themselves. But there was something more with Alma. Her protests hadn't been a test to see how he'd handle it. That answer had been too glib, Fargo reflected. He had the feeling she'd been testing herself to find out how much it'd take to control him. If so, Fargo smiled, Alma was making a mistake others had made before her.

He let his thoughts turn to Charles Dunlap and recalled how Dunlap had also been a surprise to him. The man had none of the drive and strength he'd expected to find. Indeed, he could see Charles Dunlap on the Sunday pulpit more comfortably than as a forceful land and cattle baron. The man's letter had come when the drive for Will Fowler into the North Dakota territory had ended. It had offered more than top dollar, the kind of money you didn't turn down, and he'd traveled across the border to the small house at the foot of Turtle Mountain where Charles Dunlap had been waiting. Fargo thought about that first meeting. Alma had been there, too, her long glances delivering their own message almost at once.

Charles Dunlap, a narrow-framed figure with a

narrow face to match and thinning, sandy hair, had been definite about his plans. But the man's often hesitant air didn't match his words, Fargo recalled. Dunlap spoke with a quietness, almost a diffidence as he looked out over a long, thin nose. But Fargo reminded himself he'd made no hard-and-fast judgments then, and he was making none now. He'd seen quiet, hesitant-appearing men before who hid a core of ruthless iron behind their appearance.

"The house here is just a way station," Dunlap told him. "My ranch is west of Turtle Mountain. We'll stop there, pick up equipment and some more diggers."

Fargo nodded to the three men lounging a few yards away. "Besides those three?" he asked, and Charles Dunlap nodded back.

"They're not diggers. Wilson, the tall one with the hooked nose, is my personal bodyguard. The other two help him," Dunlap said. "A man doing all the things I'm doing is always a target. He needs a bodyguard."

"Your letter said you were heading out to prospect for gold," Fargo mentioned.

"Yes, got a good lead on a place up past the Assiniboine River. I'll be more specific when we get to the ranch. I need you to find a trail that'll let me take wagons and supplies and keep my scalp on," Dunlap said.

"You've got Indian trouble up here?"

"We've got all kinds of trouble," Dunlap said with an edge of crypticness in his voice. "But you're the very best, I'm told, though I understand this is new country for you."

"Half the places I go are new country," Fargo said. "Men give names to places—America, Canada, Manitoba, Minnesota—but land is land, a trail is a trail, and an oak an oak. Mother Nature doesn't pay much mind to borders. Neither do most red men."

"I have to make a short trip in a few days, but we'll be ready to head for my ranch by the week's end," Charles Dunlap had told him, paid half the agreed-upon monies, and the meeting had ended. Alma had invited him to dinner twice, and he'd gotten a better chance to study Charles Dunlap again. The man plainly had a firm grasp of all his enterprises, but again he seemed more a bookkeeper than a man of drive and fire. But it was clear that he worshiped Alma as he deferred to her every wish and whim. On both nights, Dunlap gone to bed early and left Alma to play her own games with him, Fargo recalled. And she'd done just that until the night before, when she'd all but told him to come see her.

Fargo stretched, turned aside musings, and closed his eyes. Maybe the weeks ahead would be dangerous as all hell, but they wouldn't be boring, he wagered as he let sleep come over him.

The night stayed quiet and the cool winds blew softly until dawn broke and he rose, washed, and dressed at a nearby stream. He took the rest of the day to leisurely give the Ovaro a thorough grooming with dandy brush, body brush, and curry comb, and finishing with the hoof pick he always carried in his tack bag. When he was through, the horse glistened in the late-afternoon sun, and Fargo let him run free across a meadow of gray-green pussytoes.

When the day slid into night, Fargo relaxed against the bark of a northern balsam until the night deepened. When he swung onto the horse, he rode slowly toward the modest house that nestled at the foot of the mountain, and he saw the dim glow of light inside Alma's room. He tied the Ovaro to one side and used the rear door again to enter the darkened corridor inside. He had nearly reached Alma's room when he heard her voice, sharp with anger. "You're a rotten bastard, Wilson," Alma said. "I always knew it."

"You can call me whatever you like, Alma, so long as you pay up," Fargo heard the man's voice, and moving onto the balls of his feet, he crept forward to the door, which hung open enough for him to see into the bedroom. The hook-nosed man's tall figure faced Alma with easy nonchalance. "I saw him come in last night and I saw him leave. Now, you want to keep on having fun, you got to pay for it," Wilson said. "No money and I'll have a lot to tell your husband. I can guard his honor as well as his body, can't I, now?"

"Bastard," Alma hissed, her face drawn tight with fury. "This is blackmail."

Wilson laughed, a hard, bitter sound, and shrugged his shoulders. "Call it anything you like. Just pay me," he said. "Maybe that Mr. Trailsman will chip so's he and you can keep on enjoyin' yourselves. I'll take a down payment now. You've got some cash around her someplace."

"You can't get away with this. You can't prove anything. You didn't see anything," Alma flung at him.

"I saw him come in and I saw him leave, and in between you turned down the light. That's enough, Alma," the man said confidently, and Fargo swore under his breath. It would be enough for most husbands—and probably Charles Dunlap as well. He grimaced as he stepped forward, aware there was no way but to make the man back off.

"You're going to forget whatever you saw, friend," Fargo said, and Wilson turned, surprise flooding his hook-nosed face.

"Well, now, look at this, back for another round he is," the man sneered. "Now, the price might just go up some."

"You go to Dunlap and I'll call you a damn liar, and so will she," Fargo said. "All you'll do is get yourself fired."

The man's hook nose seemed to curve further downward as an oily smile slid across his face. "He'll believe me," Wilson said. "Specially when I tell him I had to shoot you dead because you tried to stop me from telling the truth."

"Is that what you figure to do?" Fargo asked quietly.

"Right here and now unless you and the little lady start paying up," the man said.

"Forget even trying it, and forget whatever you saw and get your weaseling, blackmailing carcass out of here in one piece," Fargo said, his voice growing harsh. He saw the man's eyes change expression, a dangerous anger flood their depths, and a split second after, the man's hand snapped upward for his gun. Fargo's Colt seemed to fly from its holster as he drew with a smooth, lightninglike motion too quick for the eye to follow. The single shot caught Wilson in the center of his chest and the man doubled almost in two as he flew backward, crashed into the wall, and fell to the floor still doubled over. He shuddered and lay still, and Fargo's glance went to Alma as he holstered the Colt. She stared down at Wilson's figure with her eyes wide.

"You shot him. You shot Charles' bodyguard," she breathed. "Oh, my God."

"Didn't plan to. He went for his gun. I'd no damn choice left," Fargo said. Alma continued to stare at the figure on the floor. "You can say he came up to attack you and you managed to call for help. I heard it and tried to stop him," Fargo said.

"No, I can't say that," Alma breathed, her eyes wide.

"What do you mean, you can't say that?"

"I can't," Alma said, lifting her face to look at him.

Fargo felt the frown dig into his brow just as he heard the sound of hoofbeats approaching outside the house.

Alma spun, ran to the window, and peered out. "Oh, God. It's Charles," she gasped. "He's come back early."

"Damn," Fargo murmured.

"You'll have to get rid of him," Alma said, and gestured to the body on the floor.

"How? Where?" Fargo snapped.

Alma stared at him, blinked, and her eyes grew wider as the hoofbeats grew louder. She shrugged helplessly.